Bridget Kavanagh, Julia Kavanagh

**The Pearl Fountain**

And Other Fairy Tales

Bridget Kavanagh, Julia Kavanagh

**The Pearl Fountain**
*And Other Fairy Tales*

ISBN/EAN: 9783337073305

Printed in Europe, USA, Canada, Australia, Japan

Cover: Foto ©Andreas Hilbeck / pixelio.de

More available books at **www.hansebooks.com**

# THE PEARL FOUNTAIN

AND

## Other Fairy Tales

BY

BRIDGET AND JULIA KAVANAGH

*WITH THIRTY ILLUSTRATIONS*

BY

J. MOYR SMITH

NEW YORK
HENRY HOLT AND COMPANY
1876

# CONTENTS.

# The Pearl Fountain.

A LONG time ago the Fairy Queen thought she would go about to see how all the fairies who live in floods, rivers, streams, and fountains were getting on since the last hundred years, for it is only once in a century that her Majesty can take such a survey of her subjects. After travelling a long time, scolding some fairies who had got into mischief,

A

and praising others who had behaved well, the Queen
came at length to an old, old forest which grew on the
very top of a rocky mountain, and where the trees were
so large and the shade was so thick that it was all green
within. Indeed it was so green a place, so dark and
so cool, that people were afraid of it, and kept aloof.
But the Fairy Queen was afraid of nothing; moreover
she had particular business in that forest. She wanted
to see a little fairy who was only three days old, and to
whom the fountain of the forest had been given by her
mother. The Queen found the little Fairy all alone
by her fountain. It was a beautiful fountain; the
water was as clear as clear could be; it came sparkling
out of a rock, leaped down other rocks, then ran away
and hid itself in the moss. It looked quite a merry
sort of fountain, and the little Fairy to whom it belonged looked every bit as merry; for when the Queen
came upon her, she was dancing in the shade and
singing to herself in a sweet clear voice, because you
see fairies can talk, just as they can run about, as
soon as they are born.

The Queen of the Fairies has no children of her own.
but she is very fond of little children, and she always

thinks the last baby she sees the prettiest. She thought so of this young Fairy, who was really a pretty creature, for she had golden hair, blue eyes, and rosy cheeks, and her mother, knowing the Queen was coming, had dressed her out in a little frock of silver tissue, shot with green and blue.

"Well, my dear," graciously said the Queen of the Fairies to this young thing, "do you know who I am?"

"Oh yes," answered the little Fairy, "you are her Majesty."

"What a clever child you are," said the Queen, quite pleased; "and who are you?"

"Please your Majesty, I am the little Fairy of the little Fountain."

"My dear, you could not have answered me better; and now what gift will you have from me, my love?"

"Pearls," answered the little Fairy.

"Then pearls you shall have," said the Queen, "as many as ever you can wish for. Your fountain shall be all pearls, and you may do what you like with them; but you will have to count them, every one."

"I shall like that," answered the little Fairy, "for no one must ever take so much as one of my pearls."

"Well," said the Queen, "if you mean to keep your pearls to yourself, you must live here all alone, and never go out."

"I shall like that, too," said the little Fairy, "for I shall sing to myself, and play with my pearls; and, please your Majesty, may I be called the Fairy of the Pearl Fountain."

The Queen let her have that also, then went her way. The Fairy of the Pearl Fountain remained in the forest, and lived there till she grew up to be the loveliest young Fairy that had ever been seen. She had a white marble basin, made for the water of her fountain to fall into, and the most beautiful wild flowers set in the green moss around it. The water sprang up in a jet from the centre of the basin, and the delight of the Fairy was to stand in the very middle of it, clothed in her robe of silver tissue, shot with green and blue, for it was not a frock now that she was grown up, and to throw the water up ever so high, till it reached the sunshine; and every drop of water she threw up was a pearl when it came down again—a beautiful white pearl. Some were big pearls and some were little ones, and the bottom of the marble basin was covered with them. Indeed, there were so many that the Fairy was obliged to let the smallest trickle away every night through a little slit in the basin; for if she had not done so, it would have overflowed. So the pearls slipped away, and rolled down the rocks on the mountain-side, but no one minded them, or if some passer-by did see them by chance, why he thought he saw drops of water and no more. Though she had so many pearls the young Fairy never thought she had too many, and all her delight was to adorn herself with them. She strung the largest and the clearest on a thread of gold, and mixed it up in her hair, and she made a necklace of more, and bracelets for her wrists, and a waist-band, and the hem of her silver tissue robe was all studded with pearls; and there was not another fairy who had so many. She counted them every one as the Queen had ordered her, and when she laid herself down on the moss at night she still counted them in her sleep. Indeed, she was so fond of her pearls, and so jealous of them, that she never left her fountain lest any one should come and steal them whilst she was away.

This lasted a long time; till one day the Fairy, finding that no one ever came near the place, and wish-

ing to go and see her sister, who lived outside the forest
in a crystal turret on a rock, and was indeed no less
than the Fairy of the Waterfall, put on her best pearls
and left her fountain for the first time.    Being a fairy,
she could go on counting the pearls of the fountain
all the same.   Well, the Fairy was glad to see her sister,
and pleased to climb up to the very top of the crystal
turret, and look down at the world below, for she had
never been out before, and she was enjoying herself very
much, when all of a sudden she cried out : " I must go ;
I miss a pearl ; no, it is not one, but two.   I declare
three pearls are gone."

"What matter about three pearls," said her sister ;
" have you not got enough ?"

But the Fairy of the Pearl Fountain declared there
was no misfortune like that of losing one's pearls, and
went away in a great hurry.   She missed two more
pearls as she walked through the forest, for she was not
one of those fairies who have only to wish themselves in
a place to be in it ; and on reaching the fountain, she
looked at once for the thief ; but she only saw a little
wren, perched on the edge of the marble basin, and
catching a drop of the spray in her bill as it fell.

"You little robber," cried the Fairy in a rage ; "is it you who have been stealing my pearls ?"

"Please, ma'am," replied the Wren, quite frightened at seeing her so angry, "I am only drinking a drop of water."

"A drop of water! don't you know, you dishonest bird, that what was only a drop of water when you drank it, would have turned into a beautiful pearl if it had fallen into the basin. Look down at the bottom and see. All these pearls were drops of water once."

"I protest, ma'am, I knew nothing of the kind," answered the little Wren, speaking very humbly, for she had never seen so grand a lady as the Fairy of the Pearl Fountain, with her beautiful hair and her pearls ; "I saw water," continued the Wren, "I was very thirsty, and I made bold to drink. Surely, I thought, the good Fairy who owns this lovely fountain will never be angry with me for taking a drop of water ; and I can assure you, ma'am," added the Wren, dropping the Fairy a curtsey, "that it was the very sweetest water I ever tasted, and I do hope you will forgive me." The Fairy of the Pearl Fountain had a hasty temper, but she was not hard-hearted ; she looked kindly down on the little

Wren, and said, "You are a silly bird, and I daresay did not know pearls from water. I suppose I must forgive you this once, but mind you never do such a thing again."

"Oh no, ma'am, never," answered the Wren very earnestly. "And please, ma'am, may I go home to the palace now?"

"Home to the palace?" repeated the Fairy. "What do you mean?"

Now every one, big or little, has a story; and the story of the Wren was this:—She had built her nest in the garden of the King's palace, and was making herself comfortable there, when the young Prince found her out, caught her, and would have killed her, if his sister had not come up in time to save her life. The Princess did more; for she took the poor little Wren, who was frightened to death, to her own room, and gave her a beautiful cage to live in, and keep her out of danger; but as the Wren is fond of going about, she let her have a fly every day, and kept a window in her room always open, so that she might have no trouble in getting in or out. All this the Wren told the Fairy, not in a few words, but in a good many; for she is a chatterbox if ever there was one, and can talk by the hour. The Fairy, however, did not mind letting her have her say; for she had got into the fountain again, and was throwing up the water ever so high, and trying to catch the beautiful pearls as they fell back. She missed a good many, for some rolled down her neck and shoulders, and others got in her hair and stayed there; and others, again, slipped through her fingers and fell into the basin.

"Oh! ma'am, how beautiful you are!" the Wren could not help saying; "and how pretty it is to see you playing with those lovely pearls."

"You have a great deal of sense," said the Fairy. "By the way, what is your name?"

"Jenny, ma'am," answered the Wren, dropping her another curtsey. "The Princess always calls me Jenny."

"Never mind the Princess," said the Fairy a little tartly; "but mind what I say. Well, then, Jenny, suppose that you and I have a game together with my pearls. I shall throw them, and you shall catch them again and drop them into the basin; and when we have done, I do not mind letting you have a drop of water to drink. You are a very little bird, and a little drop of water will do you."

The Wren asked no better than to play with the Fairy; so the game began. The Fairy caught the drops of water as they fell, and threw them to the Wren, who caught them in her bill—one after another, of course—then dropped them into the basin. The Wren was a clever bird, and played so well that she only missed three times. The Fairy was delighted and declared she had never had such fun. In short, they played till they were both tired, when the Fairy said, "There, Jenny; that will do for to-day. Drink your drop of water, and go home to the palace. You may come again to-morrow and have another game with me, but mind that you tell no one about my Pearl Fountain."

"May I not tell the Princess?" asked the Wren.

"Certainly not," said the Fairy; "if you do, I shall never forgive you; besides, I am a fairy, and I shall find it out and punish you at once."

The Wren promised not to say a word, and flew home to her cage in the palace. She was afraid lest the Princess should ask her where she had been, as

she often did ; but she had just been told by her
father that he had promised her in marriage to the
King of the Diamond Isles, and she was so full of
that, and of all the diamonds she was to have, that
she never even saw when the Wren flew in through
the window.   The Wren made as little noise as she
could, and pecked her supper quietly, though she had
never been so hungry in her life.   Water may turn into
pearls, but it is not the thing to satisfy one's appetite.

Well the next day the Wren flew to the Pearl Fountain, and the Fairy threw the pearls at her, and the
Wren caught them in her bill and dropped them into
the basin.   When she was tired she had her drop of
water, but though she asked to be allowed to bathe
in the fountain, the Fairy would not hear of it, and
was very cross with her for so much as thinking of such
a thing.   The Princess was not in her room when the
Wren flew back to her cage that day, and when she
came in the Wren had her head under her wing and
was fast asleep.

Matters went on so for a good while.   Every day the
Wren flew to the Pearl Fountain, and played at catching the pearls with the Fairy, and every evening she

flew home to her cage in the room of the Princess, who was so taken up with her wedding clothes that she never thought of asking her where she had been.

The Fairy became so fond of the Wren that she thought she would leave her in charge of the fountain, whilst she went to see her sister again. The Wren did not like being left alone, but the Fairy promised not to be long away. "I shall be back before sunset," she said, "and you can play as much as you like with my pearls, and even drink three drops of water, and all I want you to do is to stay and watch by the fountain, and if any one should come nigh it to call me three times. I shall hear you and come at once."

The Wren agreed to this, and stayed by the fountain whilst the Fairy went to see her sister. She played with the pearls till she was tired, then she drank three drops of water, then she stood on the edge of the basin, and thought how nice and cool a bath would be. The day was a hot one, the Fairy was away. "She will never know anything about it," said the Wren to herself. She spread out her wings, fluttered over the water, and had the most delightful bath she had ever had in her life. She was enjoying herself to her heart's content, and had just begun drying herself in the sun, when there came a great rushing noise which filled the whole forest. It was the King of the Fairies driving by, but the Wren knew nothing about that. She was frightened out of her wits. Indeed she lost her head entirely, and instead of calling the Fairy as she had promised to do in case of danger, she flew home to the palace as fast as ever her wings would take her, and never thought herself safe till she lay panting in the bottom of her cage. It unluckily happened that the Princess was in her room just then, trying on her wedding-dress.

"Why, Jenny," she cried, "what is the matter with you?"

"I was bathing in the forest," answered the Wren, "when there came a great noise that frightened me, so I flew home. See, I am not dry yet." She shook her wings and a beautiful pearl rolled down on the bottom of the cage.

"I declare that is a pearl," said the Princess, all amazed. "Why, Jenny, where have you been bathing, and where did you get that lovely pearl?"

"A pearl!" repeated the Wren, who did not know what to say.

"Yes, a pearl," said the Princess, who had picked it up and was looking at it, "the biggest, whitest, loveliest pearl I ever saw. Where did you get it?"

The Wren tried not to answer this, but the Princess insisted upon knowing how she had got the pearl, and the Wren did not dare to deny her. So having first made her promise that she would not mention it again, she told her all about the Fairy and the Pearl Fountain. When the Princess heard about a fountain in which every drop of water became a pearl she nearly went crazy, so eager was she to get at it. She wanted the Wren to take her to it at once, but that the Wren would not do; then she tried to coax her into stealing some of the pearls and bringing them home to her, but the Wren would not hear of such a thing.

"Well, at least I shall keep that pearl," said the Princess, and the Wren, who could not take it from her, said, yes, she might. When the Wren flew to the Pearl Fountain the next day, the Fairy gave her an angry look.

"Why did you leave my fountain yesterday before I came home?" she asked.

"I heard a great noise and I got frightened," answered the Wren.

"Why did you not call me?" asked the Fairy.

"I forgot it," replied the Wren.

"I miss a pearl," said the Fairy; "what have you done with it?"

The Wren was afraid to say the truth, so she answered, "I was playing with the pearls, when one rolled out and fell in the grass, and I could not find it again."

The Fairy could have known the truth by looking in her book, but she kept it under a stone in the bottom of her basin, and there were so many pearls on the top of it that she did not like to disturb them.

"Well,' she said to the Wren, "you have behaved very badly, and I am very angry with you; but if I forgive you this time will you do it again?"

"Oh no, indeed!" answered the Wren. So they made it up, and had a game, and were as happy together as they had ever been.

As soon as she took the pearl from the Wren, the Princess sent for the Court jeweller, and gave it to him to set, for she meant to wear it on her wedding-day. The jeweller declared that the pearl was the finest he had ever seen, upon which the Princess, instead of being glad that she had it, only thought of all the pearls in the fountain which she had not. She lay awake the whole of that night, thinking of them still; and one thing she was resolved upon when she got up in the morning, and that was to find out the Pearl Fountain, and to take some of the Fairy's pearls. " She has so many of them," thought the Princess, " that she ought not to mind my having a few ; and then what a fine thing it will be for me to be spoken of as the Princess who had so many pearls, and who married the King of the Diamond Isles ! "

The Wren was in no hurry to meet the Fairy that day. She took her fly rather late ; but the Princess, who had been watching her since the morning, followed her at a distance, entered the forest after her, and stealing behind the trees, soon found out the Pearl Fountain, and saw the Fairy and the Wren playing together. At last the Wren flew away, and the Fairy, who was tired, laid herself down on the moss to sleep. The Princess waited a while, then she stole softly on tip-toe to the edge of the marble basin, and holding up both her hands, she caught the pearls as fast as they fell. When her hands were full, she dropped the pearls down on the moss, and thought to begin again and have quite a heap of them. But the Fairy, who had been counting them in her sleep all the time, now missed them, and starting up, said angrily, " Who steals my pearls ?"

The Princess was so frightened that she had not a word to say for herself, and the Fairy said again in the same angry voice :

" What brought you here ?"

" I wanted some pearls from the Pearl Fountain," replied the Princess.

" And who told you about the Pearl Fountain ?" asked the Fairy.

" The Wren told me," answered the Princess.

" And who are you ?" inquired the Fairy.

" I am the King's daughter," said the Princess, " and I am going to marry the King of the Diamond Isles, and as your fountain is in my father's kingdom, I think you might give me some pearls for a wedding present."

" You shall not have one pearl from my fountain," said the Fairy ; " I keep all these for myself, but go back the way you came, and stand at the foot of the rock on your right hand as you leave the forest. You will see

B

pearls rolling down its sides. These you may pick up. They are small, and I do not mind letting you have them."

"May I have them all?" asked the Princess.

"Every one," replied the Fairy, "but mind it is only for this once; and though you may stay as long as you please, and take away as many pearls as you can pick up, you need never come again, for not another pearl of mine shall you get."

Though the Princess thought the Fairy very stingy not to let her have a few big pearls, she also thought that little pearls were better than none, so she thanked her, and went back the way she had come. She found the rock to her right just outside the forest, and, sure enough, there were the beautiful pearls rolling down its sides, and looking so white and clear in the moonlight. The Princess began picking them up as fast as she could. "I must have a necklace," she thought, "and as the pearls are small it will take a good many." Then when she really had enough for a necklace she wanted some for a tiara, after that she wanted bracelets, and after bracelets a waistband like the fairy's, then a trimming for her wedding dress, then pearls for rings, ear-rings,

and brooches, then more pearls for double sets of everything, then pearls to give away to her ladies, then pearls
for herself to keep ; in short, though she spent the night
gathering pearls, she had not got half enough by day-
break. She was very tired, but since she could have
pearls only this once, she thought it would be the
greatest pity in the world to go away without taking
as many as she could. So the pearls rolled down the
rocks, and the Princess picked them up, and the more
she had, the more she wished to have.

When the King heard that the Princess was missing
he was in a sad way. He asked the Wren about her,
but all the Wren knew was, that the Princess was in her
room when she went out to have her fly, and that she
was no longer there when she came back. No one else
knew anything, and only one thing was certain, that the
Princess had not spent the night in the palace. The
King, her father, was distracted with grief, and the King
of the Diamond Isles, who had just arrived in order to
marry the Princess, lost his appetite at once, he felt in
such trouble. The King sent messengers to look for his
daughter in every direction. They scoured the country,
and found her at length very tired and rather hungry,

but still picking up pearls.    When they wanted to take
her back to the palace, she said it was out of the question, and they were to tell the King that she had still
ever so many pearls to gather before she could leave the
spot.    The king was very much amazed when the messengers came back without the Princess, and told him
where they had found her, what she was doing, and
what she had said.

   "Pearls," said the King; "and what can she want
with pearls when she is going to marry the King of the
Diamond Isles to-morrow!    I must go and see about
all that myself."

   But when the King went and found the Princess, and
saw all the pearls she had gathered, and those she
was gathering still, and when she told him that if she
once left this spot she could never have any pearls
again, he began to think what a pity it would be not to
let her get as many as she could.

   "Well, my dear," he said to his daughter, "I shall
ask the King of the Diamond Isles to wait a day or two,
and in the meanwhile you may go on gathering pearls.
And suppose that for fear of accidents I should take
away these and keep them for you under lock and key."

The Princess agreed to this. The King took away all the pearls she had picked up, and there was quite a heap of them, and stowed them away in great chests in the palace. He also asked the King of the Diamond Isles, who recovered his appetite directly on learning that the Princess was safe, to wait a few days for her. The King of the Diamond Isles grumbled a little, but to please his father-in-law that was to be, he said he would wait seven days for the Princess.

But when the seven days were out, the Princess said she had not yet got pearls enough, and her father persuaded the King of the Diamond Isles to wait seven days more. And so matters went on from one seven days to another, the Princess still gathering pearls, and the King her father taking them away, and locking them up, and neither thinking they had enough, till the King of the Diamond Isles got tired waiting, and went off one morning without so much as ever saying good-bye. Indeed he went straight off to the Queen of Emeralds, whose daughter he married that afternoon. The King was vexed and the Princess felt rather sorry, but she thought she must only gather more pearls to make up for all the diamonds she had missed.  So she went on picking them up, and when she had a heap her father took it away in a great sack, and locked it up, till at length all his chests were full, and he thought one day he must see how many thousand pearls he had got.  He unlocked one chest and opened a sack, and out came ever so many drops of water, that rolled all over the floor.

"My goodness!" cried the King, "there's some mistake."

He opened the next sack; out came more drops of water.  Then the next and the next again, and all the sacks, and all the chests were full of drops of water, and in the whole of them there was not so much as one pearl.  For the pearls were pearls for the Princess only, and for nobody else.  When the King saw this, and what a mistake he had made, he got into such a rage that he had a fit, of which he died the next day.  The Princess was very sorry for her father's death, but she said the pearls were pearls indeed, and she went on gathering them at the foot of the rock.  There she stands to this day picking them up as fast as she can, and never thinking she has enough.

When the Wren flew to the forest again, the Fairy

" When she had a heap, her father took it away in a great sack "—*Page* 22

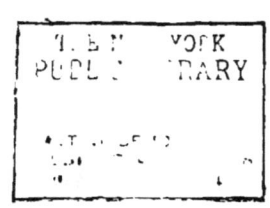

was ever so angry with her for having told the Princess about the Pearl Fountain, but the Wren begged so hard for forgiveness, and fluttered so prettily about her feet, that the Fairy said :

"Well, I shall forgive you once more, but lest you should tell tales again, you shall stay for ever in the forest with me."

So whilst the Princess is gathering pearls at the foot of the rock, the Fairy and the Wren are playing at their game with the pearls of the Pearl Fountain; and no one has ever found out in what forest that fountain is, nor on what mountain that forest grows, nor in what part of the world that mountain lies.

# The Silver Fish.

THERE was a palace once, and in the palace there lived a queen, who was called the Queen of Emeralds, she had so many of them. In front of the palace there was a large pond, and the Queen, thinking what a pity it would be to keep it empty, had it stocked with gold and silver fishes. Every one said how clever that was of the Queen, and every one was pleased save the frogs who lived in an old well in the garden behind the palace.

They were very angry, indeed, that the Queen had not put them into the pond.

"What can the Queen want with gold and silver fishes?" said a frog called Jumper. "Can they jump in and out of the water as I do?"

"Besides, they are dumb," said Croaker; "and I have a lovely voice."

"Jumping and singing are all very well," said Bulrush, the oldest of the frogs; "but what I do not like is, that the water goes from our well to feed that pond. We shall be left dry some day unless I put a stop to it."

"We wish you would, Bulrush," said all the other frogs; "you are so clever, you know."

"I know I am," answered Bulrush stiffly. "Well, don't make a noise, you young frogs; I want to think it over."

Bulrush went among the reeds and had a nap there, and when he woke, he prowled about the well till he found where the water was conveyed from it to the pond along a dark leaden tube. Bulrush was a bold frog; he floated bravely down the great rush of water, and never stopped till he came to an iron grating. The bars were too close for him to get in through, but he peeped between them, and saw gold and silver fishes swimming about in the pond. He stared at them with his big eyes till one of the young gold fishes saw him, and tumbled over on his back with fright.

"Idiot!" croaked Bulrush; but he swam back to the well, and as he had to go against the stream, he was very much out of breath by the time he got there.

"Well," said all the frogs, crowding round him; "what have you found out, Bulrush?"

"I have found out that there is nothing uglier than a gold fish," answered Bulrush, "unless it be a silver one."

"Dear me!" said the frogs; "are they so hideous as all that? But what about our business? When will you begin, Bulrush?"

"Begin what?" he asked crossly.

"Begin preventing the water from leaving our well, to be sure," said Jumper.

"Indeed!" sneered Bulrush; "and how would *you* do that, if you please?"

"Why," said Jumper, "I should stop the hole, of course."

"And the Queen would get it unstopped, and turn us all out of the well," answered Bulrush. "No, Jumper, that will not do. And now, don't make a noise; I want to think it over."

Upon which Bulrush went into the reeds, and took a very long nap there. Some busybody went and told the Queen how angry and jealous the frogs were; but the Queen only laughed, and said:

"Let them be angry; I shall do as I please."

Every day she had a large cake baked for the gold and silver fishes, and every morning she went and fed them with her own hand. When they saw the Queen standing on the edge of the pond with the cake in a basket, all the gold and silver fishes swam towards her, seven rows deep; and one little Silver Fish, the smallest of them, swam at their head and kept them in order. He hindered the big ones from pushing the little ones about; and when the little ones got rude or too frolicsome, he would just go and give them such a whisk of his tail that they were glad to dive down and hide their heads for shame. The

Queen was so pleased with this, that she said to him one day:

"Little Silver Fish, I am going to make you King of the other fishes."

"May it please your Majesty," said the little Silver Fish, very uneasy, "I would rather remain as I am; besides, the other fishes will never acknowledge me as their King."

"But they must," said the Queen; "and to show them that you are their King and Sovereign, I shall give you one of my own emeralds, and you shall wear it."

"Oh! may it please your Majesty," said the little Silver Fish, more uneasy than ever, "if the other fishes see me with an emerald and they get none, they will hate me, and perhaps take it from me."

But the Queen would have her way. She bade her jeweller measure the neck of the Silver Fish, and make him a little collar of gold thread with one of her emeralds set in it; and when the collar was made, she put it herself round the neck of the Silver Fish, and told all the other gold and silver fishes that they were to obey him, for now he was their King.

Whatever they thought about this, the gold and silver fishes were too much afraid of the Queen, and too fond of cake, to say a word against anything she might do. They cried: "Long live Silver Fish!" and bobbed before him; and matters went on just as they had gone on before. The only difference was, that the little Silver Fish wore his gold collar with the emerald at the back, for all the other fishes to know him by; and it certainly was the prettiest thing in the world to see him swimming about with that thread of gold round his little neck, and the beautiful emerald shining in the water.

The Silver Fish had been king a year wanting a day, when the Queen came one evening to the edge of the pond and said to the fishes :

"I am going away to-morrow morning early. I want to see my daughter who is married to the King of the Diamond Isles, as you know; but I have left orders to the cook to make and bake your cake every day, and to my prime minister to come and feed you every morning with his own hand."

"Long live your Majesty!" cried the gold and silver fishes.

"Will you be good whilst I am away?" said the Queen.

"Oh! so good!"

"And not push forward and fight for the largest bits?"

"Oh! never!"

"And above all things will you obey little Silver Fish?"

Obey him! why the gold and silver fishes all protested that they would die for him, nay, if he liked it, they would carry him on their backs, so that he need swim no more.

"No need for that," said the Queen; "but mind you obey Silver Fish. He is your King, and whilst he wears the gold collar with the emerald in it, the water will never leave your pond; but if any of you should try to take that collar off, the pond will run dry in no time." With that the Queen went away.

Well, the cook made and baked the cake every day, and the prime minister went and fed the fishes every morning for a week; but on the morning of the seventh day after the Queen was gone, the prime minister, instead of getting up early, said to his wife:

"I really do not see why the Queen has set me to feed fishes."

"You are a great deal too clever for it, my dear," answered his wife.

"Well, I think I am," said the prime minister; "besides, the Queen works me so hard when she is at home, that I feel I ought to have a holiday now that she is away. I want to lie in bed a little in the morning."

"Of course you do," answered his wife; "send your page Jeremy, and do not get up before eleven."

When the cook saw that it was Jeremy and not his master who fed the fishes, she thought:

"Why should these fishes have cake? bread is good enough for them; besides, I daresay that big boy eats half of it, and I am really tired making and baking a cake every day. Bread they shall have, and if they will not eat it—why they may leave it."

Accordingly, when Jeremy came the next morning the cook gave him a loaf of bread and no cake. The boy took the loaf to the pond and threw it in big lumps to the fishes, who were there as usual, seven rows deep, with Silver Fish at their head.

"I am afraid there is something wrong with our poor Queen," said Silver Fish; "this is bread and not cake—still bread is good, and we must be glad to get it."

"Bread and not cake," cried all the fishes; "we will not touch it, we will starve first."

Silver Fish tried to argue with them, and said that may be the Queen could afford cake no longer, and that bread was very good, and so on. They would not even listen to him, but all declared in a breath that they would die rather than eat bread. Jeremy went back to his master and said:

"Please, sir, the fishes will not eat. They made a great hubbub over what I threw to them; and the meaning of it all was, that they would not eat whilst the Queen was away."

"Very well," said the prime minister, who was still half asleep; "go and tell the cook that the fishes will not eat whilst the Queen is away, and that she need bake nothing for them till her Majesty comes back."

Well, when the hour at which the fishes were fed came round the next morning, they all swam to the

c

edge of the pond seven rows deep, and waited for their cake, but no cake did they get.

"I suppose we must eat bread," grumbled the older and the wiser ones, shaking their heads at the thought. But though they waited, telling each other of the good old times when fishes had cake every morning, and there was no talk of bread, neither bread nor cake did there come to them that morning. When they were tired with waiting, the fishes swam away, and when they got too hungry they swam back; and nibbled at the bread that still floated about the pond. They nibbled so well that only one piece was left, and the biggest of the gold fishes and the biggest of the silver fishes had a set battle over that last piece, whilst the other fishes looked on, and the more daring ones kept darting at it in the hope of getting a few crumbs. Silver Fish tried to keep the peace, but no one would mind him.

"Who are you, sir, to dictate to us?" asked a big fellow, giving him a push.

"Yes, who are you?" said another, swimming up to his very nose, and bobbing his big head up and down at him.

Silver Fish modestly replied that he was their King, upon which the two big fishes burst out laughing. It was no use reminding them that they had promised the Queen to obey him. One fish found out that it would have been all right if Silver Fish had been King a year; but as there wanted a day to the year when the Queen went away, he could be no King at all: and another fish said quite loud, that the best of all reasons for not minding a word Silver Fish could say was, that if their cake had been stopped, it was because he was in a league with the cook. In short, every fish in the pond quarrelled with another fish, and there was only one thing the fishes agreed upon, and it was that Silver Fish had done all the mischief.

"Hang him!" said some.

"Put him in prison," said others.

"Don't touch him," said a clever fellow, "whilst he wears the Queen's emerald. If you do she will hang us all like so many herrings."

This frightened them all. They knew the Queen was very strict, and no fish likes to be hung. No one dared to touch Silver Fish after that; and, indeed, as it was getting late the fishes gave up quar-relling for that day, and went to bed feeling both sulky and hungry.

Bulrush, who was very cunning, made no attempt against the gold and silver fishes, whilst the Queen of Emeralds stayed at home; but he set all the young frogs to gather him fine strong grasses, and when he had enough of them he made a large net. This net was just finished when the Queen went away, and Bulrush at once set to mischief. He picked up an acquaintance with that same young Gold Fish whom he had so frightened once, but who was not at all afraid of him now. They met at midnight at the grating when all the other fishes were asleep, and they plotted together against Silver Fish. The young Gold Fish told Bulrush how their cake first, then their bread had been stopped; how they were starving every fish of them; and how Silver Fish was the cause of it all.

"And what business has he to be our King?" said the young Gold Fish; "he is only silver after all, and the only gold about him is in that collar which the Queen gave him."

"If you had a bit of spirit, you would take that collar off," said Bulrush.

"We dare not," replied the young Gold Fish; "it is a gold collar, and it has one of the Queen's emeralds, and if we were to take it off, all the water would run out of our pond."

"Well," said Bulrush, "I shall tell you what to do, my friend; help me to catch Silver Fish, and I will take him away to a well, and keep him there."

"You will not hurt him!" said the young Gold Fish.

"No, no, never fear," replied Bu'rush.

"And you will not take his collar off," said the young Gold Fish.

"Of course not," answered Bulrush.

"And what shall I have for giving him up to you?" asked the traitor.

"You shall have the Queen's emerald," said Bulrush. "I was 'prenticed to a jeweller, and can take it out quite easily."

The bargain was struck, and the next thing was to know how they were to catch Silver Fish. Well, it was agreed that Bulrush should come with his net to

the edge of the pond that very night, and that when
he had thrown it into the water, the young Gold Fish
should beguile Silver Fish into it. They parted very
well pleased with each other, for the young Gold Fish
had a silver collar, which was an heirloom in his
family, and he thought how he could put the emerald
into it, and perhaps be King; and Bulrush laughed
in his sleeve, to think what faces the fishes would
make when he took off Silver Fish's collar, and all
the water ran out of the pond.

"Well, our time is come at last," said Bulrush to
the other frogs when he got home; "I have found
it all out."

"What have you found out, Bulrush?" cried the
frogs.

"Why, that there is a Silver Fish in the pond,
who wears a collar of gold with the Queen's emerald
in it, and that if we can get this collar off his neck,
all the water will run out of the pond."

"Will it?" cried the frogs. "What a good thing;
and how clever you are, Bulrush."

"I know I am," said Bulrush; "and now listen to
me." Then Bulrush told the frogs about his net,

and how the young Gold Fish was to drive Silver Fish into it.

"Silver Fish," said Jumper; "how do you know he is the right one? perhaps he is called Silver Fish because he is gold, and not silver. I say, drag the pond, and get all the fishes out."

"Yes," cried the frogs; "drag the pond, and get all the fishes out. The upstarts have been in it long enough."

"Hold your tongue," said Bulrush very sharply; "let us get Silver Fish out first, then we will drag the pond after that if you like."

All the frogs now harnessed themselves to the net, and dragged it from the well across the garden to the pond, in front of the palace. Bulrush then gave the signal he had agreed upon with the traitor, three croaks, each a little louder than the last, and immediately the young Gold Fish, who was on the watch, put his head out of the water. It was a clear moonlight night, and he saw Bulrush and the other frogs all standing in a row on the edge of the pond.

"Dear me, Bulrush," he whispered, "how many of you there are."

"The net is heavy," answered Bulrush; "so my friends have helped me to carry it."

"Dear me!" said the young Gold Fish, who began to feel uneasy; "what a large net to catch only one fish!"

"Come, no nonsense," said Bulrush; "where is Silver Fish?"

"I think I would rather not tell you," answered the young Gold Fish, diving down.

He thought to hide in a hole, and be safe there; but it was too late.

"Cast the net," cried Bulrush, in a rage, "that fish is a traitor!"

Jumper, who was on the other side of the pond, set his frogs to work, and Bulrush set his; and the net was thrown, and the pond was dragged, and the fishes, who woke up in a fright, tried to hide and could not; and they were all taken out and caught by the frogs, and thrown in a heap on the sand and gravel.

"Now," said Jumper, with a croaking laugh, "let us go home and leave these fine fellows there."

"No," said Bulrush, "that will never do; the Queen

would know what we have been about, and punish
us, for you know she is very strict. We must throw
all these fishes back again into the water, excepting
Silver Fish. He is a little fish with a gold collar
and an emerald in it: you will know him quite
easily. Bring him to me when you find him. I
wish to take his collar off with my own hands, and
to see the water run out of the pond. I think, too,
we shall leave Silver Fish out. He will die, of course ;
but then the Queen will think the other fishes have
done it, and, at all events, she cannot give him
another collar if he is dead, you know."

The frogs would rather have left all the fishes out
of the water, and killed every one of them ; but they
were afraid of the Queen. They did as Bulrush told
them, and began tumbling the fishes about and looking for little Silver Fish. Now, just fancy what Silver
Fish felt when he heard Bulrush. He was lying
under a heap of other fishes all panting, all full of
gravel, all feeling just ready to die, and all thinking
that the end of the world had surely come, when
gold and silver fishes could be so treated. Some
shed tears, some begged for mercy, some abused the

frogs, and some called on Silver Fish to help them. But Silver Fish said never a word. He covered himself with earth as well as he could, so that he was all black with mud, and that you could see nothing of his gold collar; he got on his back to hide his emerald, then he shut his eyes and stiffened himself out as if he were dead, and lay quite still. All this time the frogs were pulling the poor fishes about, looking for Silver Fish with his gold collar and his emerald, and sneering at every fish they handled.

"Go and clean yourself, my fine fellow," they said to one, as they threw him back into the water.

"Where is your gold?" they said to another, who was all gritty with sand.

"Stop," said Jumper, as he saw the young Gold Fish, who had put his silver collar on just ready for the emerald, as he thought—"stop, I say; do not throw *him* back, if you please. A gold fish with a silver collar! Here is our man."

"No, Jumper," said Bulrush; "we want a silver fish with a gold collar."

"Nonsense!" said Jumper; "they called him silver,

because he was gold; and they said his collar was gold, because it was silver."

"Jumper, I am amazed at you," said Bulrush. "Do you not see that this fish has got no emerald?"

"Well, I suppose it fell out," answered Jumper, who always would have the last word.

Now whilst Bulrush and Jumper were arguing, the other frogs had thrown back all the gold and silver fishes into the water save little Silver Fish. He was so dirty, poor fellow, that there was no knowing now whether he was gold or silver; not a sign of his collar could the frogs see for the mud; and, as he lay on his back, his emerald was hidden. The frogs could have seen it if they had turned him over; but, somehow or other, they never thought about that.

"He has no gold collar," said a frog.

"He has no emerald," said another.

"He is dead," said a third, "let us throw him in to his friends. Since they are so hungry they had better eat him."

All the frogs laughed and nudged each other, and one winked and said, "Don't hurt his feelings!"

With that they tossed Silver Fish into the water,

and stood to see him float, since that is the way of all dead fishes. But Silver Fish was not dead, and he did not float. No sooner was he in the water than he became quite lively, and swam about to clean himself. Presently his little silver coat shone as bright as bright could be, and lo! there was the collar of gold round his neck, and the beautiful emerald in it, so bright and sparkling, for it was such a lovely moonlight night that all the frogs could see it quite plainly. Well, when the frogs saw that the dead fish was a live fish, and that he was Silver Fish with the collar of gold, and the emerald in it, they were in such a rage as frogs never were in before, but the angriest frog of all was Bulrush.

"Now, you idiot!" he cried, shaking his fist at Jumper, and giving the young Gold Fish a kick, "is that Silver Fish! Come," he added, turning to the other frogs, "let us throw in the net again, and catch him!"

"Yes, yes," cried the frogs, "let us catch him, the traitor, who was alive and pretended to be dead!"

"More easily said than done!" laughed Silver Fish, diving down. And, indeed, it could not be done at

" The Queen turned out her Prime Minister at once, and gave the cook warning."
—*Page* 46.

all, for when the frogs thought to throw their net again, they found that the weight of the fishes had made a great big hole in it, and that it was worthless.

"Bulrush, what shall we do with this fish?" said Jumper, pointing to the young Gold Fish.

"Let him lie there and die!" croaked Bulrush, in his deepest voice.

"Bulrush, what shall we do with ourselves?" asked Jumper, scratching his head.

"Go home," snarled Bulrush; and home all the frogs went, leaving the young Gold Fish on the edge of the pond, with his silver collar round his neck.

And now the gold and silver fishes had got a lesson, and they begged little Silver Fish to forgive them; he did so willingly; but that gave them back neither bread nor cake, and they might have starved if the Queen had not luckily come home in time to set matters right. When she went to the pond, she found the young Gold Fish lying there in a dying state. Though much exhausted, he could still speak, and had breath enough left to tell the Queen of his treason, and of the misdeeds of Bulrush and the frogs. The Queen turned out her prime minister at once for having been too fond of lying in bed, gave the cook warning for not having obeyed her orders, and had the well stopped up, so that the frogs could never get out again, and make mischief. Bulrush died with spite, but Silver Fish was King all the days of his life.

# The Golden Hen.

GOLDEN HEN lived in Fairyland
with the Silver Peacock and the famous Blue Bird,
whom every one has heard of. These two had been
in the world, but the Golden Hen had never left home.
She got tired of living in Fairyland all the days of
her life, and one day she said to her friends:

"I too must go out into the world. I find it dull
to waken in Fairyland, to eat in Fairyland, and to
sleep in Fairyland. I must have a change."

"Take care," said the Silver Peacock; "I went into the world and I repented it."

"And you know," put in the Blue Bird, "that if you do go, you cannot come back for a year and a day."

But the Golden Hen would not be advised. She flew away out of Fairyland, and flew and flew until she came to the world at last. It was a long journey, and the Golden Hen felt very tired when she alighted upon a corn-stack. She was very hungry too and began to peck at the corn. Some hens from a neighbouring farm had been let out into the field, and the Golden Hen, who liked company, thought she would join them. After a while she flew down and pecked with the other hens, and as no one seemed to mind her, she went home with them in the evening. When the farmer's wife came out with her apron full of corn to feed the fowls, she saw this beautiful hen, and wondered where she came from; but she did not drive her away, for she thought, "She has got astray, but I shall keep her. She is a wonderful creature and shines like real gold." So the Golden Hen roosted with the other hens that night, and went out with them the next morning.

Fairy birds never lose their feathers in Fairyland, but when they leave it and choose to travel, they fare just like other birds. As the farmer's wife was looking for new-laid eggs the next morning, she saw three yellow feathers, that shone and glittered like gold, lying in the straw. She picked them up and found that they were gold indeed, and so fine and so pure that she had never seen any to compare with it. Now this woman was a great miser. She threw down her eggs for fear the Golden Hen should escape; she ran after her, caught her, and began plucking her as fast as she could and as much as she dared without killing her outright. The Golden Hen screamed and struggled, but it did not help her a bit; the farmer's wife would not let her go till she was all torn and bleeding.

"Ah!" thought the Golden Hen, "I wish I had minded the advice of the Silver Peacock, for what is to become of me, if, as the Blue Bird says, I must remain a year and a day in a world where I have already been used so ill."

After a while, however, the Golden Hen began to think that every one might not be so cruel to her as

D

the farmer's wife had been, and that she might fare
better if she went farther.  So whilst the other hens
were pecking in the stubble, she slipped away into a
little wood hard by and hid there ; and at night, instead
of going back to the farm, she went up to roost alone in
a tree, where she remained nearly the whole of the
next day.  The farmer's wife came to seek for her in
the morning, threw corn about and called her ever so
coaxingly, but the Golden Hen was not to be caught
again.  She stayed safely hidden till her enemy had
long been gone.  Then she came down and pecked a
little corn and flew up again on the least noise.

The farmer's wife came again to the wood the next
day, and the Golden Hen up in her tree thought : " Ah !
well, I shall be caught this time."  But she need not
have been so frightened.  The woman only picked up
the corn which she had scattered, and neither called
the Golden Hen nor tried to find her, for on looking
that morning at the feathers which she had plucked
from her, she had found that three only, and they
were not large ones, were gold, whilst the others were
common yellow quills.  When the Golden Hen sheds
her feathers they are real gold, but when any one

robs her of them, they are just yellow feathers and no more.

The corn being gone, the Golden Hen was nearly starved that day; she also felt rather dull, for she had always been used to company. "I cannot bear this life any longer," she thought, "I must eat and I must have society." She left the wood at once and went pecking on the way, until in the evening she came to a large farm, twice as large as the first. There were more hens than you could count in the yard of that farm, and the Golden Hen, peeping in at them through the bars of the wooden gate, thought to herself; "There are so many hens here, that if I can once get in amongst them no one will ever find me out." She waited till the henwife's back was turned, then slipped in unseen. The other hens, seeing how ill she was, were kind to her. They let her in amongst them, allowed her to feed and roost with them that night, and to go out with them the next morning.

For six days the Golden Hen remained on the farm, and no one save the other hens was the wiser for it; but on the morning of the seventh day, as the farmer watched the henwife counting the eggs, he overheard a little white hen saying: "And so you really are the Golden Hen, and your feathers are real gold. Well, to be sure, how wonderful!"

"Hush!" said a black hen, "the master is there, and you know he understands all we say."

Unfortunately for the Golden Hen, this was too true. The farmer had both heard and understood what the little white hen said, and on learning that the Golden Hen was actually on his farm, he had all the gates and doors shut, and the hens driven into a corner of the yard. He soon spied out the Golden Hen, though she tried hard to hide behind the others, and having caught her, he carried her to a room upstairs, where he began plucking her.

"Some one has been at you before me," said he, as he pulled out her quills; "but if you escaped once, my pretty hen, I shall take care that you do not escape again."

When he had plucked the poor hen almost bare, he locked her up in the room and put the key of the door in his pocket.

This farmer had a servant lad called Robin, who was both inquisitive and cunning. He had seen his master catch the Golden Hen, take her upstairs, 'and come down again without her. It so happened that Robin had a rusty old key that opened the door of the room in which the hen was locked up. As soon as his master's back was turned he crept upstairs, opened the door, and peeped in. In a moment the Golden Hen slipped out between his legs, and flew away through an open window. Robin could have caught her again, but if he had tried to do so, his master would have found out all about the key. He therefore locked the door, crept downstairs very softly, and let the Golden Hen get off. She made her way out of the farm through a hole in the hedge, and was far away when the farmer came in to feed her. He was as mad as mad could be on finding that she had escaped; but it was some comfort to him to remember all the golden feathers he had taken from her. He went to look at them at once, and instead of a heap of treasure he found ever so many yellow quills that were worth nothing at all.

The Golden Hen had enough of the world by this, and would have given anything to go back again to Fairyland; but as she could not do so till the year

and the day were out, all she thought of was to
get away from farms and farmers and farmers' wives.
She crept for a while along the hedge through which
she had escaped, then seeing that no one was by, she
got into a green field where a cow was grazing, and
from that again to other fields, till she came to one
where two little boys were gleaning. The Golden
Hen kept in the furrows so that they should not see
her, and stayed hiding there till it was evening time
and the children were gone.

These two boys were the orphan grandchildren
of a poor old widow who lived hard by, and early
the next morning they came to glean again. At noon
they sat down under a hedge, and began to eat
some dry bread. Each had a piece, a very little one,
for their grandmother was poor, and could give them
no more. The Golden Hen, who was hiding close
by, peeped at them through the hedge, and listened
to every word they were saying. They were talking
about the little sheaf of corn they had gleaned, and
rejoicing over it. They knew how glad their grandmother would be to get it, and they also hoped that
she would make them a cake with the flour.

"They are very poor," thought the Golden Hen. "I fear they will not give me any of their corn ; and they have so gleaned that there is none left ; but then they are also very little. I scarcely think they will hurt me, and if they attempt it I can hide from them." She came out of the hedge, and showed herself to the two children, but prudently kept at a little distance.

"Oh! what a pretty hen!" cried the younger boy.

"The poor hen," said the elder one, "see how torn and bare she is."

He threw her a piece of bread, but it was too near, and the Golden Hen, who was getting mistrustful, did not dare to come and take it. He then threw her another piece farther away, and this she ate greedily, for she was starving. Then the younger boy took an ear of corn, and shelling it in his hand, he scattered the grains, and the Golden Hen, getting bolder as she saw how kind the children were, drew near and pecked it before them. So they fed her till they had eaten all their bread, and then they went away to glean in other fields. The Golden Hen followed them at a distance, and picked up a little corn on her way. When evening came the boys went home, and the Golden Hen hid in a hedge, and stayed there all night.

The two boys came to glean again the next morning, and as soon as she saw them, the Golden Hen joined them. They gave her some of their bread again at noon, and this time she eat it quite tamely, pecking it out of their hands, and when they went home that evening the Golden Hen followed them. When the grandmother of the two boys saw the state the poor little hen was in, she was very sorry for her. She gave her corn to eat, and water to drink, then she stroked her softly, and having washed the clots of blood from her feathers, she gently rubbed her with a little butter, and as it was night now, and she knew that the hen would want to roost, she settled a perch for her in a corner of the cottage.

"Ah, well," thought the Golden Hen, as she flew up on the perch and roosted, "I have met with kind people at last."

Poor though the old woman was, she would not turn out the little hen, but kept her for charity's sake. "I shall not miss the creature's corn," she said; "besides, how can I let her wander about and seek for a home?

She is so ill, poor thing, that no one would have her."

"I see that I have found a home," thought the Golden Hen, who heard her. "I shall stay here till the year and the day are out, and then I can go back to Fairyland."

The Golden Hen took a long time to get well, but at length her pretty feathers all came back, and she shone so that the old woman and her two grandchildren declared there had never been a bird like this. She was a great pet with them, and never went out for fear of falling into evil hands. She did not get much to eat, for they were very poor; but she knew they did their best, and never grumbled. She had been three weeks with them when the younger boy found one of her feathers in the little yard where she used to peck alone. He showed it to his brother, who found another feather the next day. Their grandmother, not knowing that these feathers were gold, left them to the children to play with.

It so happened that as the two brothers were playing with their feathers one afternoon, a pedlar looked over the hedge and saw them. He pushed the little

wicket door open, and called out to the old woman to
come and see his wares; but he was looking at the
golden feathers all the time.

"I can buy nothing," said the old woman, coming
out, and wiping her hands in her apron, for she had
been washing; "I want nothing just now; besides, I
have no money."

The pedlar pressed her to no purpose, then after a
while he said : "Let me have these little yellow things
that your boys are playing with, and I will give them
some pretty toys instead."

As the boys asked no better, their grandmother consented to the exchange. To one the pedlar gave a
drum, and to the other a horse and car for the two
feathers.

"Have you got any more of them ?" he asked, as
he put them by.

The widow had saved up the feathers dropped by
the Golden Hen. She did not know their value, but
she thought them pretty. She replied that she had
seven more, and as the pedlar asked to see them she
went and fetched them at once. He was so anxious
to get them, that he offered her a gown for herself and

a cap for each of the boys in exchange for the seven feathers. She gladly agreed to this, and was as pleased with her bargain as the pedlar was with his. From that day forth the widow and her grandchildren saved up the feathers of the Golden Hen very carefully, and they had quite a heap of them by the time the pedlar came again. This time they all got an outfit for the winter, and a little money besides, for the roof of their cottage wanted mending sadly.

Perhaps the Golden Hen did it on purpose, but she certainly dropped so many feathers about this time that it was quite amazing, and the next time the pedlar came, the widow would take nothing but money in exchange for her little treasure. With that money she bought a cow, and rented some land, and hired a stout servant boy to till it. And still the Golden Hen dropped her feathers, and the pedlar came and bought them, and paid dearer for them every time he came, for the widow, as she wanted money less, raised her terms, and sold her feathers dearer and dearer. Well, to make a long story short, by the time summer came round again, the widow was a prosperous woman, and had begun to build a house, and she had two cows and a horse now, and hens and geese, and turkey cocks, but none of these were allowed to interfere with the Golden Hen, who still had her perch in the corner of the cottage, and roosted there alone every night.

The year and a day had been out a week, the Golden Hen was now free to fly back to Fairyland, but she liked her friends so well, that she could not make up her mind to leave them. "I shall go to-morrow," she used to say to herself, but when the morrow came, she put it off for the next day again, and so a whole week went by, and she could not find it in her heart to go. "They want some of my feathers still," thought the good little hen. "I shall leave them when the house is built."

Now, as the widow and her two grandsons were eating their dinner one hot summer's noon, the pedlar suddenly looked in at them through the open window.

"Good-day to you, ma'am," says he.

"Good-day, master," answered the widow. "I have got more feathers for you, if you want them."

"My good woman, I do not want feathers. I want your bird."

"My bird!"

"Yes, your hen. I want her, and you must sell her to me."

The widow and the two boys cried out in a breath that the hen was not to be sold.

"Well, it is no use hiding or mincing the matter," said the pedlar; "but the fact is, that the goldsmith to whom I sold the feathers, sold them to the Queen, who made a necklace of them, then a crown, and who now wants the bird, so just name your price."

The widow declared that nothing could tempt her to sell the Golden Hen, but the pedlar assured her that the Queen was bent on having her, and again bade her name her price.

"If the Queen will take my hen from me, I cannot prevent her," said the poor widow, crying, "but nothing shall ever make me sell my dear little hen."

The pedlar went away much displeased, and the widow and her two grandsons could eat no dinner, they were in such trouble. They could think and speak of nothing but the Queen and their hen, and they talked the matter over that same evening, whilst the hen was roosting.

"Grandmother," said the elder of the two boys, "let

us put the hen in a basket and go away with her, so far, so far that the Queen cannot overtake us."

"No," said his brother, "let us stay at home, and give the Queen a feather a day if she will only leave us our little hen."

The poor grandmother shook her head at all this. She knew there is no bribing a queen, and no running away from her. She also knew that queens will have their own way, and she sadly feared that the Golden Hen must be given up to her Majesty. Well, they heard no more of the pedlar. He did not come the next day, nor the next again, and on the third day the widow and her two grandsons were beginning to take heart, and to hope for the best, when the younger boy cried: "Mother, I hear a great beating of drums!"

"And, mother," said the elder one, "I hear a great galloping of horses."

"Ah!" said the grandmother, "the Queen is coming for my Golden Hen."

And so she was. The Queen herself was coming to take the Golden Hen away. Presently the drums left off beating, and the tramp of the horses ceased, and

"The Golden Hen began flapping her wings, so that a shower of golden feathers fell down on the grass below."—*Page 63.*

a gilt carriage, drawn by eight milk-white steeds, stopped at the widow's door, whilst the Queen herself alighted. She was dressed in blue satin, and had a gold necklace round her neck, and a gold crown on her head, and both were made out of the feathers of the Golden Hen.

"My good woman," said the Queen, looking very grand, "I hear that you have got the Golden Hen, and I have come for her. Where is she?"

"May it please your Majesty," answered the widow, dropping the Queen a curtsey, "I cannot part with my hen. The children will break their hearts if they lose her."

"Now do not, there is a good soul, do not go on with such nonsense," said the Queen, "but just let me see that hen of yours."

Even as she said the words, the Golden Hen, who was in the yard all the time, flew up into an apple-tree, and began flapping her wings, so that a shower of golden feathers fell down on the grass below.

"Now, that is beautiful," cried the Queen, clapping her hands, she was so pleased; "I shall die unless I get that hen. Page, go and catch her directly."

Page did as he was bid, and began climbing up the apple-tree, where the Golden Hen was flapping her wings and shedding her feathers all the time ; but just as he stretched out his hand to seize her, the Golden Hen flew away, high up into the air, where the Queen and all the courtiers saw her soaring and shining like a speck of gold in the light of the sun, until she vanished entirely.

The Queen was so vexed at not getting the hen, that she stepped back into her carriage and rode away without saying a word ; and when the drums began to beat, she made a sign with her hand that they should not.

When the widow and her grandsons were alone they picked up the feathers which the good little hen had shed, and there was quite a heap of them. The two boys were ever so glad that their hen had escaped from the Queen, and made sure that she would come back to them in time ; but their grandmother guessed, from all the feathers she had dropped before going, that the Golden Hen did not mean to return ; and she never did. On leaving the apple-tree she flew away straight to Fairyland, where she has remained ever since.

The boys were very sorry for the loss of the Golden Hen, but they were comforted in time, and, thanks to her parting gift—for the Queen bought all the feathers, and paid handsomely for them—they were rich farmers when they grew up.

E

# Sunbeam and her White Rabbit.

was so
called
because
she had
golden
hair that
flowed round
her face, and

made it as bright as the sun on a summer morning. No
one could see her and not feel glad, and when she went
to the village on an errand for her father and mother, who
lived a little way off, every one welcomed her; and it
was: "Good-morning to you, Sunbeam." "How are you,
Sunbeam?" or, "I am so glad to see you, Sunbeam."
And yet Sunbeam was only a poor man's child.

Her parents lived in a little cottage in a wild waste
place, almost surrounded by rocks. Sunbeam was fond
of climbing up there, and as she sat amongst the wild
flowers, she liked to watch the bees looking for honey.
She was not afraid of them, and they knew her quite
well, and liked to see her there. Sunbeam was sitting
thus one day with the bees around her, when a Big Bee
said to her,—

"Would you not like to stay with us, Sunbeam? It
is very pleasant up here with the wild thyme and the
blue bells, and all that."

"Yes, it must be nice," replied Sunbeam; "but you
see I must go home to father and mother."

"Well, I suppose you must," said the Bee, after con-
sidering a while. "I don't remember my father myself,
but I was very fond of my mother, as nice an old bee as

ever you saw, Sunbeam, and the best mother in the world. But as I said, it is very pleasant up here, and we have a very good hive in that old oak, and plenty of honey in it, I can tell you."

"Yes, it must be pleasant in the old oak-tree," answered Sunbeam ; "but then how could I get in ?"

"I am afraid you are too large," answered the Bee, after looking at Sunbeam. "Well, never mind, my dear, it is no sin to be big, and we like you all the same."

"Thank you," said Sunbeam ; "but what noise is that which I hear below ? "

"Oh! that is the Giant hunting. He is a dreadful man—he spoils all our flowers with his hounds and horses. I cannot endure the sight of him."

So saying, the Bee flew away in a pet. Sunbeam looked down in the plain below her, and watched the Giant riding by on his big black horse. He looked so terrible, and he was so tall, that Sunbeam felt quite afraid of him, and hid low among the rocks lest he should see her. But he did not, for the Giant, the hunts-men, and the hounds were all pursuing a poor grey rabbit and her young one, who was white as milk. The grey rabbit flew across the plain and was caught and killed; but the little White Rabbit climbed up the rocks and jumped right into Sunbeam's lap. She took him in her arms and ran home with him, and the Giant, the huntsmen, and the hounds were so glad to have caught the grey rabbit that they never missed the white one.

Sunbeam was very fond of her White Rabbit. She made him a bed of moss and fern, and worked him a pretty red collar and a pair of red garters, which she put on him every morning. She took him with her whenever she went to sit among the bees in the rocks. Indeed, the bees and the White Rabbit became very good friends. They did not mind his skipping about, and kindly gave him up the wild thyme to nibble when they had sucked and done with it. When Sunbeam went to the village, the White Rabbit followed her, walking very nicely on his hind legs, and "Sunbeam and her White Rabbit" became a byword, for you never saw the one without also seeing the other. So sure as Sunbeam appeared with her golden hair, so sure the White Rabbit was behind her.

Now it so happened that the Giant, who was getting old, could not go out hunting any more, and fell into very low spirits. He had heard of Sunbeam and her

White Rabbit, and he thought he would like to have her.

"I find that this castle of mine is getting very dark," he said to his wife; "go and fetch me Sunbeam. I am sure she will make it quite bright again with her golden hair. I shall also like to put my hands through it, and see if it is gold. Besides, she has got a White Rabbit, who will skip about the room and make me laugh, for I have heard that he walks on his hind legs, and he can dance, I daresay; and when I am tired of him I can have him dished up for my supper."

The Giant's wife was a good woman, but she was mortally afraid of her husband, and would not have disobeyed him for the world. She went at once to the little cottage in which Sunbeam's parents lived, and she said to them quite politely, for she was a very civil lady—

"If you please, where is Sunbeam?"

"May it please your ladyship, Sunbeam is out," answered Sunbeam's father.

"Ah, well," said the Giant's wife, "send her round to me as soon as she comes home. My husband finds that his castle is getting very dark, and he is sure Sunbeam will make it quite bright again with her golden hair. He will also like to put his hands through it, and see if it is gold. Besides, Sunbeam has got a White Rabbit, who will skip about the room and make him laugh, for he has heard that he walks on his hind legs, and he can dance, I daresay."

But the Giant's wife said nothing about having the White Rabbit dished up for the Giant's supper. The parents of Sunbeam were in sad distress at having to give her up to the Giant ; but they did not dare to say no. They knew besides that it would be of no use, for if the Giant had set his mind on having Sunbeam, why have her he would. They promised to send her up to the castle when she came home, and on that promise the Giant's wife left them.

When Sunbeam came home that evening her mother had not the heart to send her to the castle.

"Let us keep her this one night more," she said to her husband ; and he answered, "Yes, let us keep her this one night more."

"Sunbeam," said her mother to her, "you must get up early to-morrow. The Giant is ill, and you will have to take some new-laid eggs to the castle."

"Very well, mother," answered Sunbeam. She did not mind going to the castle if the Giant was ill, for she made sure that she should not see him. Sunbeam slept in a little cot, and the White Rabbit's bed of moss and fern was close to it. They both went to bed as usual, and Sunbeam soon fell fast asleep, but the White Rabbit did not. Towards midnight, when everything was very quiet in the cottage, he got up on Sunbeam's bed, and gently scratched her face with his paw. Sunbeam woke at once, and saw him in the moonlight, which was shining brightly through the window.

"Well," said Sunbeam, "what is it? Are you thirsty? Shall I give you a drink?"

"I am not thirsty, thank you," answered the White Rabbit; "but don't talk so loud, Sunbeam, for I have got something to tell you. If you take new-laid eggs to the Giant's castle to-morrow, the Giant will keep you. He finds his castle getting very dark, and he is sure you will make it quite bright again with your golden hair. He will also like to put his hands through it, and see if it is gold. He wants me to skip about the room and make him laugh, for he has heard that I can walk on my hind legs, and he fancies I can dance ; and when he is tired of me he can have me dished up for his supper." For the White Rabbit could not merely talk, he also knew everything.

. "Oh, what shall we do !" said poor Sunbeam, who began to cry. " I shall die with fright if the Giant puts his hands through my hair to see if it is gold, and I shall break my heart if he has you dished up for his supper."

" Don't cry, Sunbeam," said the White Rabbit, " but do as I bid you. Get up as soon as it is dawn, and open the door as softly as you can. We will go to the rocks and hide there, and take my word for it the Giant shall not find us."

Sunbeam did as the White Rabbit told her. She got up as soon as it was dawn, dressed herself, put the White Rabbit's red collar and garters upon him, then opened the door as softly as she could. Neither Sunbeam's father nor her mother heard her, and Sunbeam and the White Rabbit went up to the rocks together, and hid there with the bees. Sunbeam told them her trouble, and asked them to hide her and the White Rabbit, but the Big Bee answered—

"We would hide you if we could, Sunbeam, for we like you ; but you are too large to get into our hive in the oak, you know."

"That is very true," said poor Sunbeam, crying; "I wish I were not so big."

"Don't cry, Sunbeam," said the White Rabbit, "it will all end well; take my word for it."

Well, when the father and mother of Sunbeam awoke, and found that Sunbeam and her White Rabbit were gone, they were in sad trouble, for they thought how angry the Giant would be. And he was in a fine way indeed, and sent all his dogs and all his men to fetch Sunbeam. "Mind you bring me back Sunbeam," growled the Giant, as he sent them, "and her White Rabbit as well. I want to hang him with one of his own red garters."

Neither the dogs nor the men could find Sunbeam and her White Rabbit at the cottage.

"They are with the bees," said one man, "let us go and look for them up in the rooks."

Now when Sunbeam heard the dogs, and saw the men coming for her, she wrung her hands, and cried bitterly.

"Oh! what shall I do if they get me," sobbed poor Sunbeam, "I would rather be that bee than go to that wicked Giant's castle, and have him putting his hands through my hair to see if it was gold."

"Would you," said the White Rabbit, "and what should I be then?"

"Why, you could be that pretty little ant close by."

Well, the dogs now smelt the White Rabbit, and began to bark, and the men saw Sunbeam, and cried out to one another: "There she is," "We have got her." But when they came up to the spot where Sunbeam had been, the child was gone, and all they saw was a little golden bee humming above the wild thyme.

"I'll kill that bee," said one of the men in a rage; but just as he was going to fling his cap at the poor little bee, an ant stung his foot, so that he screamed with pain. Up and down among the rocks went the dogs and the men, but neither Sunbeam nor her White Rabbit did they find, and the Giant had to do without them.

The father and mother of Sunbeam were very glad

that she had escaped, but they wondered what had become of her. They were afraid she was hungry, and they went and looked for her among the rocks with some bread and milk in a basket, which Sunbeam's mother carried, but no Sunbeam with her White Rabbit did they see, and when they called her no answer did they get. Then Sunbeam's mother began to cry. " I am afraid our little Sunbeam is lost," said she.

" I am afraid she is," answered her husband ; "yet let us hope, wife. The White Rabbit is very clever; he will take care of her."

When they were tired looking they went home and went to bed, for it was night, and each dreamed of Sunbeam that night.

" Wife," said Sunbeam's father, when he woke the next morning, " I dreamed that I saw our Sunbeam among the rocks, sucking the wild flowers, and the White Rabbit was with her."

"Yes," said his wife, "and she was saying, 'I wish I had some honeysuckle,' and the White Rabbit answered: 'Tell your father to get you some.'"

" Then I will," said Sunbeam's father.

He took some honeysuckle from his little garden, and set it among the rocks, and the next night both he and his wife dreamed of Sunbeam, and they saw her sucking the honeysuckle, and laughing, and looking as bright as ever.

Well, days, weeks, and months passed, and nothing was seen or heard of Sunbeam.

Her father and her mother dreamed of her every night, and she looked so happy that they became comforted, the more so that the Giant was always sending his wife to know if Sunbeam had come back, because he found his castle getting darker and darker, and he wanted Sunbeam more than ever.

" Better have our Sunbeam anywhere than with the Giant," said Sunbeam's father.

" Ay, better indeed !" said his wife.

They both died when Sunbeam had been gone seven years. The Giant's wife died too, and the Giant, who was more wicked than ever, was left alone with his grandson the Prince. He was called the Prince because his mother had been a princess. He was a very handsome young man, rather tall, but not a giant, and as good as his grandfather was wicked. The

Giant, not having been able to get Sunbeam with her golden hair, had got together all the gold he could lay his hands on instead. But though he had so much gold that his castle was almost full, he found it getting darker and darker every day.

"I have not gold enough," said the Giant; "but how am I to get more? I am too old to fight now, and the Giantess, who has twice as much gold as I have, would not marry me. Perhaps she would marry Prince, and come and live here, and bring all her gold with her."

The Giant went and asked the Giantess, who was his fifth cousin, if she would marry his grandson, and bring her gold with her. The Giantess lived in a castle hard by, and received her cousin very kindly. She agreed to marry Prince, though she found him rather short. "But then," said she, "we can put him upon stilts!"

"And you will bring all your gold," said the Giant.

"To be sure I will," replied the Giantess, "and tell Prince to get a pair of stilts and practice walking with them, so that he may be quite steady on the wedding-day."

The Giant went home and asked for Prince, but the young man was out.

"Where is he," growled the Giant.

"May it please your Giantship," answered one of his men, "Prince is up in the rocks. Prince goes there every day."

"Does he," said the Giant, with a big frown, "well, tell him to come and speak to me as soon as he comes in."

Prince was up in the rocks, as the man had told the Giant. He liked nothing so well as being there, for as he sat resting there one day, he had amused himself with watching a little yellow Bee, as bright as gold, and very pretty, that went about humming among the flowers, and what struck Prince much, was that wherever the Bee went a little brown ant followed and went too. When he came again to the rocks, a few days after this, Prince saw the golden Bee and its little brown ant again, and, indeed, day after day he saw these two, and they knew him as well as he knew them. One morning the Bee was humming around his head when Prince said to it:

" Come on my hand, Bee."

Immediately the little golden Bee alighted on his finger, whilst the ant stood still under a blade of grass, and waited. Prince was very much pleased to see the Bee so friendly.

" I wish you could talk, Bee," he said, " and tell me what I could do to please you."

But the Bee only gave a little hum, and after a while flew away. Immediately the ant moved on, and soon the two were gone. Now, this happened the very same day on which the Giant went to see the Giantess.

"Where have you been," growled the Giant, as soon as the Prince came in.

" I have been to the rocks," answered Prince.

" Well, then, you will not go there to-morrow," growled the Giant again. " You will have to go and court the Giantess, whom you are going to marry, and mind you get a nice pair of stilts in order not to be too short for her."

" Marry the Giantess," cried Prince, in a rage at the thought ; " never."

" And I say you shall marry her," growled the

F

Giant; he was always growling since he had lost his teeth.

"But why should I marry her?" asked Prince.

"Because she has ever so much gold, and that I want gold," answered the Giant. "Gold is yellow, and I like it."

"And I saw a yellow Bee to-day in the rocks," answered Prince; "it was as yellow as gold, and I like it."

"A Bee," sneered the Giant; "perhaps you want to marry that Bee."

"I would rather marry her any day than the Giantess," answered Prince, quite angry.

"A Bee is it?" cried the Giant, in a passion; "well, then, you shall marry that Bee, and Sunbeam's White Rabbit shall be your bridesman."

What put Sunbeam's White Rabbit into his head just then was more than any one could imagine. Perhaps it was because Prince had come from the rocks where Sunbeam and her White Rabbit had been so fond of going formerly.

"Marry the pretty little Bee I saw to-day," answered Prince, laughing; "well, I ask no better, and I shall be glad to see a White Rabbit."

The Giant stamped his foot and shook his fist, but Prince would not marry the Giantess—they were a stubborn family—and the long and the short of it was that the Giant said Prince should marry the Bee, and that Prince answered, he asked no better.

In order to scorn his grandson the more, the Giant had a day appointed for the wedding of Prince and the Bee. He sent out a great many invitations, and they were all accepted, for every one wanted to see a Bee married. The Giantess, however, was too much affronted to come, though she only pretended to laugh, and asked if Prince meant to wear the Bee in his bonnet. The Giant also had presents prepared for the bride, a gold crown and necklace, and wedding clothes made for a good sized Bee; the wedding dress was gold brocade, as stiff as stiff could be. The marriage was to take place up in the rocks, and there, on the wedding morning, the Giant went with Prince, who looked very handsome in white satin, and forty fiddlers walked behind them, all playing, and as many lords and ladies as could be got together, and all so beautifully dressed that every one agreed there had never been a wedding so grand as was this. Prince walked first, and as soon as he got up in the rocks, the little golden bee came towards him, and lit on his finger.

"Oh! that is the Bee, is it?" said the Giant.

"Yes," answered Prince, "that is the Bee."

"And what White Rabbit is that behind you?" asked the Giant.

The Prince turned round and saw a White Rabbit in a gold collar and garters.

"That is my bridesman," he answered.

"Well, then," said the Giant, "will you marry that Bee?"

"Yes," answered Prince, "I will."

"And you, Bee, will you marry Prince?" asked the Giant.

"Yes," answered the Bee, "I will."

And scarcely were the words spoken when Sunbeam appeared before them in the stiff gold brocade dress, and with the gold necklace and the crown of gold on her beautiful sunny hair.

Every one was amazed and every one was glad. The forty fiddlers began to play, and Prince took Sunbeam straight home to the castle, with the White Rabbit

" The forty fiddlers began to play, and Prince took Sunbeam straight home to the castle.'
—*Page* 84

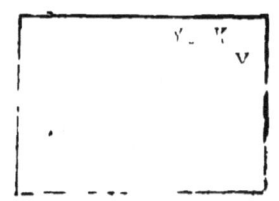

walking on his hind legs behind them, and a swarm of bees went with them as far as the castle gate, but would not go in for fear of accidents, though Sunbeam, who was grateful for the kindness they had shown her so long, pressed them ever so much.

"Thank you, Sunbeam," said the Big Bee; "but our oak-tree was too small for you formerly, and your castle is too large for us now. So good-bye, and come and see us." With which the Big Bee flew away with all the other bees after her.

The Giant was so pleased to have Sunbeam at last, that he declared he did not care for the Giantess and her gold now that he had Sunbeam and her golden hair. Sunbeam agreed to let him look at it as much as he liked, provided he did not put his hands through it.

The Giant promised that he never would, but made it a condition that the White Rabbit should wear his gold collar and garters and dance for him every evening. This the White Rabbit agreed to; but he made it a condition that the Giant should never have him dished up for supper. When all this was settled the wedding went on quite merrily, and every one was as good and as happy as every one could be for ever after, especially Prince and Sunbeam; and Sunbeam never forgot how kind the bees had been to her, but often went to see them with her White Rabbit behind her.

# Redcap's Adventures in Fairyland.

EDCAP was the only child of a widow who lived by sifting the corn which the farmers brought to her. She threw away the bad seeds outside of her door, and they fell in the earth and grew there, so that after a time her little house was almost hidden in a grove of blue, red, white, and yellow flowers that smelt so sweet and were so pretty to look at, that it was quite a pleasure to see them. Redcap liked the red flowers best, and he always stuck one or two in his cap, and that was how he came to be called Redcap. All these flowers bore so much seed that birds flocked to the place and built their nests near it. They sang all the day long in spring, and chattered all the year round, and there was nothing Redcap liked so much as looking at the flowers and listening to the birds. He only wished he could know what they said when they talked to each other; and at length he asked the Magpie, who was the greatest chatterer of all, and was always going from one bird to another with his head on one side, and ever such a knowing look.

"Dear me," answered Magpie, "I wonder you don't understand them, Redcap; it is as plain as A B C, and they are all talking to you. 'Go to the Queen,' they say. 'Go to the Queen, Redcap.'"

"Do they," said Redcap—"Then, Magpie, I see what it is, I am to be a general—I always liked red— and I must go to the Queen and tell her so."

"Then I shall present you," said Magpie; "the Queen

is a very intimate friend of mine, a good soul, a very good soul is the Queen."

"Magpie," answered Redcap, "you shall stay at home, if you please. What has a bird like you to do with queens and generals!"

"Oh, ho, my fine fellow," cried Magpie, "do you think you can prevent me from going to see the Queen. Mind my words, Redcap, I shall be at court as soon as you are."

He flew away, and getting all the other birds around him, he told them how Redcap was going to court in order to become a general, and how he, Magpie, would present him to his friend the Queen.

Redcap got up very early the next morning to go to the palace, which was a long way off. He put three red flowers in his cap out of compliment to the Queen, and he stole so softly out of his mother's little house, that he made sure Magpie could not see him. When he got to the palace and asked to speak to the Queen, the porter at the gate inquired into his business.

"I want to become one of her Majesty's generals," answered Redcap.

The porter laughed, and calling an usher, he told

him what was Redcap's errand. The usher laughed, and went and told the Queen that there was a little boy at the gate of the palace with three red flowers in his cap, who wanted to become one of her generals.

The Queen laughed, and said, "Show him in."

As Redcap entered the room where the Queen sat on her throne, Magpie alighted on his shoulder, and perching there, said in his ear:

"Don't be afraid, Redcap, I shall talk to the Queen. May it please your Majesty," he began.

"Let the boy talk, Magpie," said the Queen.

"May it please your Majesty," said Redcap, "I always liked red, and I want to become one of your Majesty's generals."

"I am very much obliged to you," answered the Queen, "and I am sure you will make a very great general indeed, but you must wait till a vacancy occurs. Good-bye, Redcap."

With that she nodded to him, and told the usher to show him out, and give him some lollypops. Redcap went home with Magpie on his shoulder, talking all the way.

"Well, Redcap," said he, "I told you that I would

present you to the Queen, and you see all that has come
of it. You are to become a general, and, in the meanwhile, you have got a lot of lollypops."

"Do you mean to say that you had anything to do
with it ?" cried Redcap.

"Now, Redcap," said Magpie, "you know she was
looking at me all the time !"

"She was looking at the red flowers in my cap,"
answered Redcap, "and I don't think she even saw
you."

"You are very saucy," said Magpie, "and very
ungrateful; but never mind, I shall be kind to you for
all that."

With that he flew away, and getting the other birds
around him, he told them what fine things he had been
doing for Redcap, with the Queen.

Redcap thought to be appointed a general the next
morning or so, but when a whole week passed, and he
heard nothing about a vacancy, he could not help saying to Magpie, with whom he had made it up: "The
Queen is not making a general of me, are you sure it
was 'Go to the Queen' that the birds were saying?"

"Of course it was," answered Magpie, "and they are

saying it still; but there are more queens than one, and, between ourselves, I think they must have meant the Queen of the Fairies. I have never seen her, but I know," said Magpie, winking knowingly at Redcap, "that she is dying to see me, and so I will present you, as a matter of course, and show you the way to Fairyland."

"Thank you," said Redcap, "but I shall present myself to the Queen; and as to the road, I know very well that Fairyland lies beyond a mountain which grows close to my mother's house, and I shall get in somehow."

"Oh! ho!" cried Magpie, "you think you can do without me, do you? But I can fly, and you cannot; and I shall be in Fairyland as soon as you are. Good night, Redcap. So there is a mountain which grows close to your mother's house, is there? Well, I never heard of mountains growing before." And Magpie laughed as he flew away.

Early the next morning, long before daylight, Redcap got up, and stole out of his mother's house, making sure that Magpie could not see him. But though he went round and round the mountain, not a cranny through which he might get in could Redcap find. At length, when it was day, he climbed up in a tree which

grew high up in the mountain-side, and when he got up
on the very topmost bough, he saw Fairyland all below
him.　He also saw the Queen, who was going out hunting, riding on a white horse, with all her gentlemen and
ladies about her, and Redcap thought he had never
seen such a fine sight.

"That's the Queen," said Magpie.　"Bless her
Majesty, how well she looks!"

Redcap looked up, and there was Magpie perched
on his cap, and flapping his wings at the Queen of the
Fairies.　Redcap tried to get him off, but he thereby
loosened his hold of the tree, and down he tumbled
straight into Fairyland.

"There!" said Magpie, when he got up, "I told you
I should show you the way to Fairyland. This way,
Redcap," he added, strutting on before him, "shake
the dust off you, my boy, and don't be afraid. I shall
present you to the Queen, and do all the talking."

"May it please your Majesty," he began, going up to
the Queen of the Fairies.

"Let the boy speak, Magpie," said the Queen;
"what do you want, Redcap?"

"May it please your Majesty," said Redcap, "I

always liked red; and I want to be one of your Majesty's generals."

"Oh! by all means," answered the Queen; "but you must first change your cap. Give Redcap a cap," added the Queen, addressing the fairy on her right; "and take him to the stables," said she to the fairy on her left, "and let him choose a horse to his liking. For before I make a general of you, Redcap," said the Queen, "you must follow the hunt with me."

So one fairy gave Redcap a cap that fitted him beautifully, and the other took him to the royal stables where Redcap chose a little black horse, called Swift. The fairy warned him that Swift was rather dangerous, but Redcap answered that he liked a horse of spirit, and had him brought out at once. When he got into the saddle, Magpie perched on his shoulder, and said, quite loud:

"Don't be afraid, Redcap. If that little fairy horse should be vicious, I shall tell you how to manage him."

Swift, on hearing this, was very much affronted, and snorted and tossed his head angrily.

"Let him feel your spurs," said Magpie.

Redcap did as he was bid, and off went the little

fairy horse with Redcap on his back, and Magpie on Redcap's shoulders. Swift went like the wind, and Redcap was rather afraid, but Magpie flapped his wings, and screamed with pleasure, and cried out :

" Faster ! faster ! I say. Keep up with the Queen, Redcap ! Don't let any one get ahead of you. Let Swift feel your spurs, I say."

Redcap spurred Swift, who went faster and faster, but who, instead of following the Queen, galloped with all his might towards a large pond ; and when he reached it stood still. The pond was full of golden fishes, who all put up their heads and looked out of the water to see Swift, Redcap, and Magpie.

"Don't be afraid, Redcap," said Magpie, " I shall manage him. Come, my fine fellow," he added, alighting on Swift's head, " I shall let you see who is master ! Clear that pond, I say."

Swift on hearing this kicked up his heels, and flung Magpie off his head, and Redcap off his back. Magpie flew away, but Redcap fell right into the water. His cap got off his head and floated, and Redcap jumped into it at once, for the cap being a fairy cap was as good as a boat. On seeing him in his cap, all

the gold fishes burst out laughing, and called out
"Redcap! Redcap!"

"Never mind, Redcap," said Magpie, who had
perched on a tree ; "we shall pay these fairies out yet."

When the gold fishes heard this, they set up a great
cry, and went and complained to the Queen that Magpie had threatened them.

"Did he?" said the Queen; "then turn him out."

Magpie was accordingly turned out of Fairyland at
once.  He went back to the other birds, and told them
that the Queen of the Fairies had consented to make
Redcap one of her generals on his recommendation,
and that she had appointed him her ambassador, and
that he had so much to do, that he should never get
through it.  Redcap was very glad to be rid of Magpie, and he asked the Queen to let him mount Swift
again, and follow her.  The Queen said yes, and gave
him a little whip.

"Just touch Swift with that," said she, "and he
will carry you safely ; and now let us all be off again."

So away went the Queen, and all her ladies and
gentlemen after her, and Redcap with the rest.  But
though Swift seemed to behave very well, he owed

Redcap a grudge on account of Magpie, and as he ran he asked all the fairies on his way to rid him of that nuisance on his back. They were willing enough, for they saw how much the Queen was taken with him and his red cap, and they were already jealous of him. Swift, who was full of tricks, pretended to be taking Redcap to the pond again, but Redcap said very sternly, "Not there, if you please, sir."

Upon which Swift turned right round, and what should Redcap see before him, and between the Queen and the hunt, but a field full of eggs white as snow, and lying as thick as thick could be. Redcap reined in, for he did not know what to do. If he rode through the eggs what a mess he would be in, and if he did not, how could he keep up with the Queen? Swift, on seeing him puzzled, was so glad that he threw back his ears and laughed.

"Oh! ho!" says Redcap, "is that it? then go on, sir, and eggs or no eggs, follow the hunt, I say." He gave him a touch of his whip. Swift stooped his head and dashed through the eggs, and in a moment every egg got a pair of wings and flew away, calling out—
" Redcap! Redcap!"

**G**

"Well, Redcap," said the Queen when he came up to her, "how are you getting on?"

"May it please your Majesty," said he, "all the fairies turned themselves into eggs to prevent me from keeping up with your Majesty, and when I rode through them, they flew away and called me Redcap."

"Dear me," said the Queen, "I see you have got enemies. Take this sword, and when you are attacked, defend yourself with it. And now let us be off again."

Away rode the Queen and Redcap after her. He did not spare Swift, but made him keep up with the Queen, and Swift was more angry than ever, and told all the fairies on his way to rid him of Redcap. But Redcap was so brave that the fairies did not know what to do against him. They put their heads together, however, and presently Swift took Redcap through a field full of beautiful red flowers. Redcap was sadly tempted to get down and pick some, but he thought better of it, and only made Swift go faster. Then all at once a bee flew out of every flower until the air was thick with bees. Turn where he would, Redcap met nothing but bees. They buzzed so, that he was almost deaf, and they shed such a yellow dust that he was almost blinded. Swift, seeing him so puzzled, threw back his ears and laughed.

"Oh! ho!" said Redcap; "these must be the enemies against whom the Queen has warned me."

He took out his sword and cut right and left around him, upon which all the bees kissed their hands to him and flew away, calling out—"Redcap! Redcap!"

When Redcap got up to the Queen the hunt was over, and the Queen asked him why he had not kept up with her.

"May it please your Majesty," he answered, "I was beset with fairies under the shape of bees, who buzzed at me and shed their dust upon me, and when I cut through them with the sword your Majesty had given me, they flew away calling out Redcap."

"Well, Redcap," said the Queen, "I see you have too many enemies to stay here. You must go home for seven years, and then come back to me. Swift shall take you to the borders of Fairyland. Mind you do not lose your cap, your whip, or your sword. Good-bye, Redcap."

The Queen gave him a nod and rode away, and Swift took him at once to the borders of Fairyland

When they came within view of the tree from which Redcap had tumbled, there arose a great wind.

"Take care, Redcap," cried Magpie, who was perched on the tree watching for him; "you will lose your cap if you don't mind."

When Redcap looked up and saw Magpie flapping his wings at him, he was so enraged that he took out his sword and threatened him with it; but unluckily in taking out his sword he dropped his whip, and in stooping to pick up his whip with the point of his sword, he let his cap fall off his head. He jumped down to get it back again, but no sooner did Swift feel him off his back than he snorted, kicked up his heels, and galloped away, carrying off the sword, of which the hilt had caught in his bridle. Redcap ran after him, but there was no overtaking Swift, who only laughed and called out "Redcap!" So Redcap turned back to get at least the cap and whip, but they too were gone.

"The fairies came and took them away," said Magpie from the tree. "I screamed at them, and I flapped my wings, but they took them all the same. If you had minded me you would not have lost your cap! Well, well, better luck next time, and another time too, do mind me, Redcap."

With that Magpie flew away, and went and told all the birds how Redcap had come back from Fairyland without his cap, his sword, or his whip, and all that because he would not mind him.

The first thing Redcap did when he got home was to get another cap, and the next, to try and hunt away Magpie ; but Magpie would not be driven away. He was fond of Redcap, he said, and would be kind to him all the same. So he came year after year, chattering with the other birds, and telling them all the grand things he had done for Redcap.

Although he had lost the cap, whip, and sword, which the Queen had given him, Redcap greatly wished to go back to Fairyland. He went to the mountain and climbed up the tree, and looked down, but though he saw Fairyland very plainly, it seemed further away than the first time, and he did not dare to drop into it. Indeed, every time he went and looked at it, Fairyland got to be farther and farther, and at last it was so far that Redcap went no more, but was content to sift corn with his mother. He

would have been quite happy with the flowers and
the birds if it had not been for Magpie. When he
grew up, he built himself a big house, and stayed
almost always within it, in order to have nothing to
do with Magpie; but it was no use, Magpie peeped in
at him through the windows, and screamed and flapped
his wings, and called out "Redcap."

So Redcap had to bear with Magpie after all, and
after a time he did not mind it.

# Fire and Water.

FERN had two brothers, Fire and Water.
She was reared with Water and loved
him dearly, for he was frolicsome, and
leaped about her, and laughed, and sang :

and Fern, who was always in a sort of dream, sat in the shade, and listened to him, and looked at him through her half - shut eyes, and thought him, in his blue coat shot with green and trimmed with silver, the handsomest lad that had ever been. But Fire had been reared by his uncle, Sultan Sol, at the other end of the world, and Fern was grown up when she saw him first. She thought she must have fainted at his appearance, she was so frightened, for Fire had red hair to begin with, and the most angry-looking eyes.

"Oh! don't come near me; pray don't!" cried poor Fern, "or I shall die."

"Wait, my dear," said Fire, taking a pair of blue spectacles out of his pocket and putting them on; "my uncle Sultan Sol gave me these for fear of accidents."

"Yes; but don't come near me," still cried Fern, shrinking in horror. "You wear a scarlet coat, and scarlet is a colour I never could bear."

Fire did wear a scarlet coat lined with gold, and he thought it very fine; but he wished to please Fern, so he said again:

"Wait, my dear, my uncle Sultan Sol gave me a cloak, that is the very thing. Just see."

So saying, he took a brown cloak out of his pocket; for it was so soft and so fine that he could make it up ever so small, and spreading it out, he put it around him.

"That is my smoke cloak," he said; "but to tell you the truth I only put it on when I am out of temper. So pray do not ask me to wear it often. Well, now that it is on, you do not see my scarlet coat, do you?"

"Oh! yes, yes, I do," replied Fern, shuddering, "pray get another cloak, this is too thin."

"Oh! I can make it as thick as I like," replied Fire; "only, the thicker it is, the more ill-tempered I feel."

"Never mind," said Fern, "I cannot bear the sight of scarlet."

Fire frowned and looked quite angry; but he did thicken his cloak, and so it thickened and thickened till it looked almost black.

"Well, I suppose you will let me kiss you now," said he, going up to Fern. But she uttered a little cry.

"Kiss me!" she said; "do you mean to scorch me up?"

Fire, who was always ill-tempered when he had his brown smoke cloak on, did not mind her a bit, and was going to take her up in his arms and kiss her, when Water leaped on his back,—he liked a practical joke,—and clapped his arms around his neck. Now, Water was always cool, and if there was a thing Fire hated.

it was cold, besides people so rarely took liberties with him that he now got angry with his own brother.

"Let me go, will you," he cried, foaming and hissing with rage, "let me go, or I shall make you repent it."

"I am not afraid of you, old fellow," said Water, laughing, and giving him a sly kick in the ribs. "You cannot do anything to me, you know."

Fire tried to shake him off, but he could not; then he thought to take off his spectacles and burn him up with his angry eyes; but Water had a little squirt ready for him, and Fire put his spectacles on again in a hurry. Then he attempted to pull off his cloak, but Water breathed upon it so that the cloak grew thicker and thicker, and Fire had scarcely breath left to cry out:

"I say, do you mean to smother me?"

This sobered Water, who let Fire go, and declared he meant it all as fun. The brothers became friends again, but Fern would not let Fire come near her, and though she agreed to love him, she informed him that it must be at a distance.

"Well, then," said Fire, "I think I shall travel, and see the world a bit."

"So will I," said Water. "You will not mind my leaving you, Fern, will you?"

"Oh no," answered Fern, "I shall not." To say

" They were so frightened at the sight of the Dragon, that they wanted to run away."

—*Page* 116.

the truth, she was rather pleased that both her brothers should go away for a while. She could not help being afraid of Fire in her heart, and Water had become troublesome of late, he had such high spirits.

The two brothers agreed to travel together, and Fern, still sitting in the shade, wished them a happy journey, and promised to wait for them there, and not marry till they came back.

"Suppose we get you a husband, Fern," said Fire, who was good-natured, and liked his sister, "a fine bright young fellow, ever so lively?"

"No, no," said Water; "Fern wants a cool, steady man; don't you, Fern?"

"You know nothing about it, either of you," said Fern saucily; "I want the Wise Man."

"What makes you want him, Fern?" asked Water.

"Well, I want him because he is wise, and I am foolish," replied Fern; "besides, I have heard that he lives in a wonderful place, and I have a fancy for a house of my own. It is very pleasant, no doubt, to live as I do; but I should like shelter in winter, and shade in summer."

"And when we have got the Wise Man, Fern," said Fire, "are we to bring him to you, or to take you to him?"

"I don't know," answered Fern; "but I do know that I shall not stir. I have never walked one step, and I am not going to begin now, am I? I was born sitting, sitting I will live, and sitting I will die."

Well, Fire and Water again bade Fern good-bye, and went on their way. They promised Fern that they would look for the Wise Man, also that they would not quarrel; but the brothers had not walked half a mile when they began to disagree. It was all about the Wise Man, and where he was to be found.

"I know," said Fire; "my uncle, Sultan Sol, has a brass palace on the top of a burning mountain, and I feel pretty sure the Wise Man lives there. Let us go to it, and take this path to the right."

"No, no," said Water, "he lives in a clear glass house on a green island. I have seen the place again and again, and this road to the left will take us to it in no time."

"As if a Wise Man would live in a glass house," sneered Fire.

"Why not as well as in a brass palace on the top of a burning mountain?" asked Water, getting angry.

In short, the brothers had a quarrel, and only agreed in one thing, and that was to part company. Fire took the path to the right, and Water the road to the left, and each turned his back on the other.

"Don't get into trouble," said Water, nodding over his shoulder at Fire as he walked away. "You are a very mischievous fellow, you know, Fire."

"Not half so mischievous as you, with your sly, quiet ways," answered Fire, blazing up; "so don't you get into trouble, brother Water."

"No fear of that," replied Water; "I do good."

"And so do I," retorted Fire; and so they went on quarrelling until they were out of sight and hearing.

Well, they did get into trouble, both of them, for they were mischievous when they meddled, and this was the way of it. Fire walked on until towards night (and a very cold night it was), he came to an old tumble-down house just outside a town—for Fire likes town much better than country. This house belonged to a Miser, who lived in it alone with his little grandchild. Fire pushed the door open, and walked into the kitchen. He found the Miser there sitting staring at the grate where two or three bits of coal were just going out, and his grandchild crouched in a corner, and crying with the cold.

"What is that child crying for?" asked Fire.

" Children are always crying," answered the Miser.

" That child cries because it is cold," said Fire.

" How can I help its being cold?" answered the Miser.

" Make those coals burn," said Fire.

" I can't," said the Miser; "the bellows wants mending."

But it was not true, he only wanted to spare the coals.

" I shall make them burn for you," said Fire. He opened his mouth, and there shot up such a blaze as you never did see, and Fire got into the blaze, and roared up the chimney, shouting Hurrah! He got out at the top, and leaped about the roof; and presently the house, which was old, began to burn. Fire laughed to hear it crackle and to see it shrivel up, and he never thought of the child. He only thought what rare fun this was. He soon found out, however, that fun gets people into mischief. The Miser's house kindled the house next it, and that lit another house, and so on; and though the Miser's house was the only one that was burned down, all the people of the town agreed that Fire was a mischievous fellow, and turned him out, warning him never to show his face there again.

For a long time after parting from his brother, Water

met no one. and he felt rather dull ; but at length, as he was walking by a little stream, he saw a Bridegroom who was going to fetch his bride. " Good-morning," said Water, " we are walking the same way, I believe. I shall be glad of your company, master."

" I daresay you will, if you get it," answered the Bridegroom, " but I want none of yours ; I am going to fetch my bride."

" Oh ! then I must go with you," said Water ; " I want to see the bride."

The Bridegroom laughed, and looked quite scornful. See his bride indeed !

" Why, surely," remarked Water, " a cat may look at a king ! "

" As to that," replied the Bridegroom, sneering, " we shall pass by here on our way home from church, so if you will wait till we come back, you may look at the bride, and welcome ; but you shall not come with me."

Water was very much affronted, but he did not pretend to be so, and merely saying he would wait, he sat down on a big stone nigh the little stream, whilst the Bridegroom got into a boat, and rowed himself across. At the end of an hour or so, there was a great sound of music, singing, and laughing, and

Water saw the bridal party on the other side of the stream. The bride was beautifully dressed, with a wreath of flowers on her head, and the Bridegroom walked by her side, as vain as a peacock. When he saw Water he nodded and laughed.

" You may look at the bride now," said he.

" Thank you," answered Water.

The Bridegroom handed the bride into the boat, and she sat down; but just as he was going to get in and sit down by her, the stream swelled and swelled until it became a river, and the boat, with the bride in it, went sailing down, and was soon out of reach. The Bridegroom stamped, and tore his hair. The bridesmaids screamed, and every one ran up and down shouting, and still the bride and the boat went floating down till they came to a mill, and were stopped by the miller. The stream was so swollen, however, that the Bridegroom had to go down ever so far before he could find a bridge, and join his bride. He shook his fist at Water, he was in such a rage, but "Good-bye," said Water, and he went away laughing.

Fire and Water had a good many other adventures of the same kind whilst they were looking for the Wise Man. They meant no harm, yet they always got into mischief, and the last trouble they had was the worst oi all. It so happened, that after going round the world, the two brothers came back to the very spot where they had parted, and that whilst Fire entered a forest at one end, Water got into it at the other. Fire had not walked long before he met a hare running for her life.

"What is the matter?" asked Fire.

"The Deer is hunting me," said the Hare, and she was gone.

Presently the Deer came running by, and Fire asked him what was the matter.

"I am hunting the Hare," answered the Deer; "and the Fox is hunting me."

After another while the Fox went past.

"What is the matter?" asked Fire.

"I am hunting the Deer," said the Fox; "and the hounds and the huntsmen are hunting me.'

And he, too, was gone.

Then came the hounds and the huntsmen; and when Fire asked them what was the matter, "We are hunting the Hare, the Deer, and the Fox," said they.

"Then I shall hunt them with you," said Fire. "Look, and see what I can do!"

With that he opened his mouth and breathed, and he shook his hair, and presently the branches of the

H

trees began to kindle, and after a while the forest was in a blaze.

Now Water, after resting some time near an aqueduct which crossed the forest, was going on again when he heard a great uproar.

He looked, and saw the Hare running and panting.

" What ails you ? " said he.

" Oh ! " answered the Hare, " the Deer was hunting me when Fire came and set all the forest in a blaze, and now we shall all be burned to death."

Then the Deer came up with the tears running down his cheeks.

" We must all die," said he ; " it is no use going away." And he laid himself down.

Then came the Fox.

" We shall be burned alive," said he. " I do not care for the hounds now."

Then the hounds and the huntsmen, barking, shouting, all came on together, and all gathered in one spot, because there was no going any further through Fire having hemmed them in.

" Oh ho ! " said Water ; " you are at your tricks, are you, my lad ? Wait a bit ! "

With that he got on the aqueduct, and opened it everywhere, till the river that was within came out and spread over all the forest, and Fire had to put his smoke-cloak on as fast as he could. But as the river spread and spread and got higher and higher, the Hare, the Deer, the Fox, the hounds, and the huntsmen all cried out, "We shall be drowned. You are worse than Fire. Let us out—let us out!"

But Water only said, "Don't be afraid!" and he walked away.

He had not walked far before he met Fire, and said to him, "Well, old fellow, you have been at your tricks again ; but I have settled you."

"You have settled the Hare, the Deer, the Fox, the hounds, and the huntsmen," answered Fire, "and you ought to be ashamed of yourself."

Upon that they had another quarrel, and they only made it up when they heard a great hue and cry behind them. They looked, and saw the Hare, the Deer, the Fox, the hounds, and the huntsmen all pursuing them, for they had escaped somehow, and they had agreed to hunt Fire and Water and kill them if they could. Fire and Water had now to run for life, and they ran till they were far out of the forest, and they came to a cavern, where they got in to hide. At first they saw nothing, it was so dark, but after a while they were aware of a little man who sat on a

stone with a big black dragon at his feet. They
were so frightened at the sight of the Dragon that
they wanted to run away, but the little man called
them back.

"Who are you?" he asked.

"We are Fire and Water," they answered. "And
who are you?"

"I am the Wise Man."

Fire and Water were very glad to have found the
Wise Man at last; but they did not dare to go nearer
to him on account of the Dragon.

"Don't be afraid of him," said the Wise Man; "I
have only just finished him, and he will not stir hand
or foot. He is the finest Dragon that ever was, but
he is also the laziest. I have coaxed him, I have
threatened him, I have just given him a whipping, and
he will not stir. I wanted him to take me about, for
I am tired of being here, and as you see, I harnessed
him to a nice little car, in which I was to sit, but if he
will not go, what am I to do?"

"Does he bite?" asked Water.

"Bite! I tell you he will not stir."

"I shall make him stir," said Water.

"Yes," said Fire, "I think we can make your Dragon
gallop if we set about it."

" He had promised to build her a beautiful palace all of glass."—*Page* 118

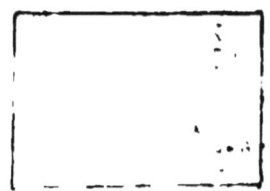

Water went and opened the Dragon's back, and got inside of the beast, and shut himself up again. Then Fire leaped on the Dragon's neck, and taking hold of his horns he urged him to go. At first the Dragon would not stir, but looked blacker and more sulky than ever. Then when he felt Water within him, and Fire on his back, he got angry. His big eyes glowed like two coals, and he bubbled and hissed and spluttered till even the Wise Man kept at a distance from him; but neither Fire nor Water were afraid. Water stayed within him, and Fire worked his horns, till the Dragon could bear it no longer, and with a great snort, and the smoke and steam coming out of his nostrils, darted out of the cavern.

"Stop, stop," cried the Wise Man, "don't go without me."

He had only time to jump into his little car, for once the Dragon was off neither Fire nor Water could stop him, when they were out scouring through the country. As they flew along they met the hunt still in pursuit of the two brothers. On seeing Fire, the huntsmen raised a great cry, and urged their horses; but Fire gave the alarm to Water, and the two managed the Dragon so well that the Hare, the Deer, the Fox, the hounds, and the huntsmen were out of sight in no time.

Fern was terribly frightened when she saw the black Dragon, and Fire getting off his back, and Water coming out of his inside; but when the Wise Man stepped out of his little car and praised her brothers for the clever way in which they had managed his big black Dragon, Fern was better pleased. Still she could not agree to marry the Wise Man till he had promised to build her a beautiful palace all of glass, which he did without loss of time. When the palace was built the Wise Man put Fern in it, and took her away in his little car. Water got inside the Dragon, and Fire on his back, and off they went again, and from that time forward Fire and Water agreed.

# Tipsy's Silver Bell.

HERE was once upon a time a poor widow who had three little boys. Their names were Dick, Jack, and Bill. They were all born on the same day, and were very much alike, for they all had curly brown hair, blue eyes, and

round rosy faces. They lived with their mother in a
poor little house, which was the very last in all the
town; but which the widow kept so neat and clean
that it was a pleasure to see it. There were plenty of
fairies in those days, and they liked best such people
as were tidy in their ways. The widow knew this and
did not let her boys forget it.

"Keep yourselves nice," said she to Dick, Jack,
and Bill, "and the fairies will surely be kind to
you."

The widow lived by sewing; but though she rose
early, worked hard all day, and went to bed late, she
found it so hard to make both ends meet that, when
her boys were only six years old, she prenticed them
all three—Dick to a tailor, Jack to a shoemaker,
and Bill to a saddler. The boys slept at home, but
went together every morning to their masters, who
lived in the same street, and were next-door neigh-
bours. Every one wondered at the widow for setting
her boys to work whilst they were still so young, and
everybody laughed at her as well; for, as these wise
people said: "Who ever heard of prenticing boys of
six?"

But though they were very young, the widow's boys were quick; and before the first year of their apprenticeship was out, Dick had made a little coat about the size of my hand, and Jack and Bill a pair of shoes and a saddle to match. The widow was so pleased, and so proud as well, of this coat, pair of shoes, and saddle, that she hung them up in her window so that every one who went by might see them. Many people stopped to look at them, they were so pretty; but every one agreed that the coat and the pair of shoes would fit none but fairies, and that none save a fairy horse could ever wear that saddle. Even the masters of the boys grumbled so at these little things, saying they were only nonsense, that the widow took them down and hid them away out of sight.

The day that she put them by was a half holiday, and the three brothers spent it at home. They made a large kite, and asked their mother if they might not go and let it fly in some fields just beyond their house. She said they might, provided they did not attempt to enter the forest. That forest had a bad name in the town, and these boys were afraid of it.

They promised not to go near it, and went off to fly their kite. At first it would not rise, because there was no wind at all; but presently there came a strong breeze, and the kite went up, up, till all of a sudden the breeze became a gale, which snapped the cord out of the hand of Bill, who held it. Away flew the kite, and away ran the three brothers after it. The kite, however, rose higher and higher, until at length it entered the forest; and before the boys had thought about it, they were in it too.

"Oh, dear!" said Dick, "we had promised mother not to do it."

"We did not mean it," said Jack.

"Yes," said Bill; "and since we are in, and are sure to be scolded, let us get the kite if we can." So they followed the kite, which went sailing along between the trees, till it got caught in the topmost bough of an old oak that grew close to a large pool of water. There was no getting at the kite there, and the forest looked so dark and wild that the three brothers, who felt afraid, were thinking of going home at once, when they heard the sound of a little bell in the distance. It came nearer and nearer, and presently they saw running towards them a little greyhound white as milk, and who was the most beautiful creature they had ever set their eyes on. He wore a gold collar round his neck, and fastened to the collar was a silver bell, which made the sweetest music in the world. It tinkled as he ran; and the day, which had been so black and stormy, became all bright with sunshine; the whole forest was lit up and looked green and gold; every bird began to sing; and, what was more wonderful, all the creatures of the forest began to talk, and the three brothers understood what they said.

"Is that Tipsy going by?" asked the little Squirrel, who was perched on a bough cracking his nuts there.

The Rabbit, putting his head out of his warren, replied:

"It is Tipsy; don't you know him by his silver bell?"

"Ha, ha!" laughed the Fox. "Tipsy's silver bell is loose; he will drop it presently."

"Dear me!" cried the Magpie; "what will Fairy Prince do then? He will not be able to get home

to-night, and the Queen will be so angry; and, you
know, he can never find the bell himself."

"Never mind," said the Lizard; "Dick, Jack, and
Bill will tell him all about it."

"As to that," said the Hare, running by, "I could
tell Fairy Prince."

But all of a sudden the silver bell ceased to tinkle,
the forest became dark again, the birds left off singing and the creatures talking, and all was just as
it had been before.  Presently tramp, tramp, and a
handsome gentleman in green and gold came riding
by.  He looked in a great hurry, and was all but
breathless.

"Boys," said he, "have you seen my greyhound?
He is white as milk, and he wears a gold collar with
a silver bell to it."

"He has just gone by," answered Dick.

"He took that road," said Jack.

"And his silver bell is under that hawthorn bush,"
said Bill, who saw it shining in the grass.

The Fairy Prince stooped and picked up the silver
bell.  The moment it tinkled the forest lit up again,
the birds sang and the creatures talked, and the beau-

tiful greyhound, who had vanished, came running back to his master, who fastened the bell to his gold collar once more.

"And now, boys," said he, turning to the three brothers, "tell me what gift you would like to have and you shall get it; for I am Fairy Prince, and this is my dog, Tipsy."

"I should like to make such a handsome little blue velvet coat, that the like of it had never been seen," said Dick.

"And I the most beautiful pair of little red boots," said Jack.

"And I the prettiest little yellow saddle," said Bill.

They all spoke in a breath, without taking time to think, and when they had said their say, all the creatures in the forest—the Squirrel, the Rabbit, the Fox, the Magpie, the Lizard, and the Hare, burst out laughing, and said, "Oh! you silly, silly boys, is that all you ask from Fairy Prince?"

"Never mind, boys," said Fairy Prince very kindly, "it is a good wish, and you shall have it; but if you want me again, come here, take a pebble, and just throw it into the water of that pool; and now good-bye to you for the present."

He rode round the hawthorn bush with his dog Tipsy. The boys heard a little plash in the water, and not a sign of Fairy Prince, of his horse, or his dog was left after that, and the moment the bell ceased to tinkle the day became dark, and the forest was as it had been before.

The three brothers, who felt rather frightened, got out of the forest as fast as they could, and after agreeing not to tell their mother what had happened to them, they went straight home.

The widow always sent her boys up to bed in the dark, for fear of fire; but when they went up that evening to the garret where they slept all in one bed, they found a bright light burning in a little lantern, and they saw on the bed a piece of blue velvet, a red morocco skin, and yellow leather, with gold thread, and lace, and needles, scissors, and an awl, and a last, and everything in short which they needed to make a coat, a pair of boots, and a saddle. They saw that Fairy Prince had not merely sent those things there, but that he meant them to set to work at once, and so they did, and sat up all night, and never left off till each had finished his task, and Dick had made the loveliest blue velvet coat, all laced and embroidered, and Jack the most beautiful little red boots, stitched with gold thread, and Bill the handsomest little yellow saddle that had ever been seen. The brothers were so pleased with their work that they all three said, "We must show it to mother, and tell her how we met Fairy Prince and Tipsy in the forest."

But when they went down, they found that the widow had gone to the well for water, and as they were rather late, they went off to work without waiting for her.

When the tailor saw the little blue velvet coat which Dick had made, he was both amazed and delighted : the shoemaker went into raptures over Jack's pair of little red boots, and the saddler shook hands with Bill, said he was proud of him, and that there had never been anything like the little yellow saddle. Indeed the tailor, the shoemaker, and the saddler thought so much of the work of their little prentices, that without having said a word to one another, they sent the coat, the pair of boots, and the saddle to the palace, each making sure that the Queen would buy them, and that his fortune was made.

"Dear me, what pretty little things!" said the Queen. "I never did see anything so pretty; but they are so little that I really can do nothing with them. Take them back to the tailor, the shoemaker, and the saddler, and say that I don't want them."

When the little Princess heard this she began to cry. "I want the little coat, the little boots, and the little saddle," she said; "I want them for Puss and my little wooden horse."

"Then, my dear, you shall have them," said the Queen. She had only this one child, who was a cripple, and could neither walk, nor sit up, nor do anything but play with her cat all the day long. The most famous doctors had not been able to cure her, or do her any good, and the Queen, who loved her beyond anything else in this world, always let her have her way, and gave her everything she asked for.

When the little Princess heard that she was to have the coat, the pair of boots, and the saddle, she left off crying, and called her cat.

"Come here, Puss," said she, "and put on that coat."

Puss came, the little Princess put the coat upon him, and at once he sat up as straight as an arrow.

"Puss, hold out your left hind paw," said the little Princess.

Puss held out his left hind paw, and his little mistress put one of the red boots on him, and it fitted beautifully.

"And now let me have the other paw," said the little Princess.

Puss held out his right hind paw, and as soon as the boot was on, he began to dance on the carpet so prettily that there never had been anything like it.

"Would you like a ride, Puss?" said the little Princess, fitting the yellow saddle on the back of her wooden horse, who, the moment it was on him, began racing round the room. When Puss saw that, he leaped up on his back and rode him, and the two, the cat and the wooden horse, galloped round and round till the little Princess clapped her hands, she was so glad, and the Queen laughed so that the tears ran down her cheeks; she was laughing still, when

I

an old lady, who was also very wise, came into the room.

"Ah! what a pity," said she, when she saw what was going on; "if your Majesty had only put that coat on the Princess, and these boots on her feet, they would have fitted her, and she would have been well at once. As to the saddle, the worst horse that ever was would have become the best in the world if he had only had it on his back; and now they will never fit any one but the cat and the wooden horse."

"I wish I had known that," said the Queen. "Tell the tailor, the shoemaker, and the saddler to make me another coat, pair of boots, and saddle directly. The coat and the boots will be for the Princess, and as to the saddle, we will try what it will do for Dobbin, who has been worth nothing for ever so long."

The masters of the three boys were delighted when the orders came from the palace, and they set their prentices to work at once. Dick, Jack, and Bill asked no better, they made sure that what they had done once they could do again, and they cut up the velvet and leather which their masters found them without

a bit of fear; but somehow or other the coat. the
boots, and the saddle they made now were not at all
like those they had made in the night, and they were
so slow about them too that the Queen sent three
times to know if she ever was to get these things.
The masters declared, all three, that the boys were
lazy, and sending word to the widow that she was
not to be uneasy about her children, they kept them
and made them sit up all night. The boys worked
very hard indeed, and at length the coat, the pair of
boots, and the saddle were finished by the morning,
and taken to the Queen, by the tailor, the shoemaker,
and the saddler.

But none of them would do. The Princess could
not get her arm in the sleeve of the coat, nor her
feet in the boots, and the saddle could never be
strapped to Dobbin's back.

"Take the trashy things away," said the Queen, in
a rage, "and let me have a coat, a pair of boots, and
a saddle like the first, or I shall make you repent
it."

The three masters said never a word, they were so
frightened; but each, when he got home, threatened

his prentice to keep him on bread and water until he had done the Queen's bidding. The boys did their best, but try as hard as they could, they only spoiled cloth and leather. Upon this the masters put their heads together, and after declaring that their prentices had never made the coat, the boots, and the saddle which had taken the Queen's fancy, they agreed to lock them up, and not give them a bit to eat till they had confessed the truth, and said who had made them.

Now this took place in the tailor's house, and Dick, who had overheard every word, slipped out, and went and told his brothers.

"What shall we do?" said Jack.

"Go to the forest and tell Fairy Prince," said Bill.

Off to the forest they went. When they came to the pool, they none of them wanted to throw the pebble in. Dick said he was sure his mother would not like it; Jack said he was afraid; and Bill said he would not. At length they agreed that each should take up a pebble, shut his eyes, and throw it in at the same time with the other two. So said, so done; each took up a pebble, shut his eyes, and threw the pebble in, and the very moment the pebbles plashed into the water the boys heard the little silver bell. They opened their eyes, and there was the forest, all lit up so beautifully, the birds singing, the creatures talking, and Tipsy going by, and Fairy Prince riding after him.

"Well, boys," said he, "what do you want?"

The three brothers told him their trouble, and asked to make another coat and saddle, and another pair of boots, like the first.

On hearing this, all the creatures in the forest burst out laughing, and cried out in a breath:

"Oh, you silly, silly boys, is that all you ask from Fairy Prince?"

"Never mind, boys," said Fairy Prince kindly, "you shall have your wish, and I dare say you will know better another time."

So saying he rode away, with Tipsy before him; and the moment Tipsy's silver bell left off tinkling, the forest became dull and silent again.

The three brothers went home very well pleased, "for now," said they, "we shall get out of trouble;" and so they did after a fashion. They made such a coat, such a pair of boots, and such a saddle, that the first were nothing to them ; and the best of it was, that the moment the little Princess put on the little coat she sat up, and was as straight as straight could be ; and that as soon as the boots were on her legs, she jumped down on the floor and began to dance, so that all the courtiers declared there had never been anything like it. The next thing she did was to ride Dobbin, whom the saddle fitted beautifully, and who, from a little vicious brute, became the best and liveliest pony that had ever been seen.

The Queen was delighted, and wanted to make the tailor her prime minister, the shoemaker her lord chancellor, and the saddler commander-in-chief of all her armies ; but, on second thoughts, she resolved not to do so till they had made her another coat, saddle, and pair of boots, for fear anything should happen to the first. And now the troubles of Dick, Jack, and Bill all began over again. They had only asked for the gift of making once these things which the Queen wanted, and when they attempted them again they were just as unsuccessful as they had been before. They did not wait, however, for their masters

to starve or lock them up this time, but went off to
the forest at once, in order to ask Fairy Prince to
get them out of trouble again.  When they came to
the pool they picked up three pebbles, and threw
them in without shutting their eyes, for they were not
frightened now; but though the pebbles went in with
a plash, there was no tinkling of the silver bell, no
Tipsy, and no Fairy Prince riding by; but instead
of these, a sound of voices, coming nearer and nearer,
and calling them by their names.

"I am sure that is my master's voice," said Dick.

"Let us throw stones in again," said Bill, who also
heard the saddler.

And Jack, who was sure that he heard the shoemaker put in his word, said, "Let us throw bigger
stones this time."

So they picked up the largest stones they could find,
and threw them in with a great noise, hoping that Fairy
Prince would hear and come to them.  But no Fairy
Prince appeared, and instead of him they saw the tailor,
the shoemaker, and the saddler coming up panting, for
they had run after their prentices all the way from
town, and being fat men, they were very much out of

breath. When the three masters saw the boys, they raised a shout of triumph, and cried out to one another :

" I see them ;" " Here they are ;" " Now we have them ;" " Hurrah ! hurrah ! "

They rushed on, striving who should be first.

" Take my hand," said Dick to Jack.

" Take my hand," said Jack to Bill.

The tailor, the shoemaker, and the saddler came on, waving their caps, and still crying " Hurrah ! " and Dick, Jack, and Bill jumped straight into the water, and were seen no more.

The three masters stood and stared at each other. Then they called to the boys, asking them to come out, and promising not to starve or beat or ill-use them in any fashion ; but either Dick, Jack, or Bill did not trust them, or they could not get out of the pool as easily as they had got into it, for they did not appear, and after agreeing never to tell any one what had happened, the tailor, the shoemaker, and the saddler went back to town very much crestfallen.

When the Queen found they could not make her the things she wanted from them, she said it was because they were stubborn and lazy, and she sent them to prison to be kept there on bread and water till they should obey her. As they were unable to do that, they might have spent the rest of their days in jail, if the Queen had not died, and the little Princess let them out on the day of her coronation.

When the widow learned that her boys had run away, and that no one knew what had become of them, she was so unhappy that there is no telling of it. She went about looking for them everywhere, and asking all the people she met if they had seen Dick, Jack, or Bill; but no one could give her any tidings of them, though she went to many strange countries, and questioned all the wisest people in the world. At length, after wandering about several years, she found a little wise old man, who said to her :

" Go home and look for your boys within a mile of your own house."

Though the widow was as tired as could be, this comforted her greatly, and she went home as fast as she could. Her way lay through the forest, but as she was afraid of it, she was going to walk round, when she met a pretty little old woman, who said to her, " Better go through the forest if you want to see your boys again."

The widow's fear all vanished as she heard this. She went into the forest at once, and walked up and down the whole day long, but not a soul did she see, nor a sign of her boys did she find. At length, being fairly tired out, she sat down by the side of the pool to rest a while before going home. She had not been sitting there long when there came up a little boy with a rod and basket. He took no notice of the widow, but began to fish. He was a very handsome boy, and looking at him, the widow was reminded of her own children, and could not help crying.

" What ails you ? " said the little boy.

The widow told him how she had lost her boys and was seeking for them, but could not find them nor learn where they were.

" They are serving their apprenticeship in Fairy-land," said the little boy, when he had heard her out ; " and they will never be able to get away out of it unless they find Tipsy's silver bell."

On hearing this the widow cried more bitterly than

"Tramp, tramp, and a handsome gentleman in green and gold came riding by."
—*Page* 124

ever, and said now she knew that she should never see her boys again.

"You can see them," said the little boy, "if you will do what I tell you."

"And what is that?" asked the widow.

"You must take my hand and shut your eyes, and not open them till I bid you. Then whomsoever or whatever you see, you must not say one word."

The widow promised to do as he bade her. The little boy took her hand, she shut her eyes, and plash! they both went into the water; but the widow was so frightened at this that she opened her eyes at once. In a moment the little boy was gone, and she was sitting alone by the side of the pool.

She stayed till nightfall, hoping he would come back, but he did not. She went home at last, but early the next day she was in the forest again, seeking up and down for a token of her boys. She found none, and when she was so tired out that she could not walk a step further, she sat down by the side of the pool to rest. Presently the pretty little boy came with his rod and basket, and began to fish. He took no notice of the widow, and it was just as if he had never seen her before. Seeing this, and also thinking of her boys, the poor woman began to cry. The little boy at first did not mind her, but at length he asked what ailed her, and when she told him, he promised to let her see her boys, provided she did not open her eyes till he bade her, and did not utter a word, good or bad. The widow promised everything, and this time she kept her word ; for though when he took her hand and jumped with her into the water she heard it plash over her head, she never opened her eyes till the little boy said to her,—

"Look now, and mind what I told you."

The widow looked as he bade her, and she found that she was standing outside a window, and that she could see through the glass in the room within. Her three boys were sitting there together, very busy working. They were fresh and rosy, but did not look a day older than when they left her. Dick was making a tiny coat of scarlet cloth, laced with gold ; Jack was finishing a little high-heeled shoe of white satin, the other stood made on the table by him ; and Bill was stitching a little buff saddle, so very small that the widow wondered for what horse it could be meant.

Presently a door opened and a little gentleman strutted in. He went up to Dick, and seemed to be saying : " Well, sir, is that coat ready?" Upon which Dick rose and tried the coat on him, and the widow saw that it fitted beautifully. Then another door opened, and a little lady with a long train came sweeping in. She went up to Jack, and he showed her the shoe. She sat down at once, and he put the shoe on her foot, and worked hard away at the other one. Then the little lady and the little gentleman got into conversation, but he was looking at his coat in a glass all the time, and the lady was peeping down at her foot. But this was not all. Bill, having finished his saddle, got up and went out of the room. He left the door open, and his mother could see a little groom holding a little horse outside. The horse, though small, was very beautiful. He was cream-coloured, and had a flowing mane and a long tail ; but he was also a spirited thorough-bred horse, and he tossed his head and pawed so that the groom could scarcely hold him. When Bill approached and tried to put the saddle on his back, the horse reared and plunged so that the widow cried out: "Take care, Bill!"

No sooner were the words spoken than all vanished,
and she found herself once more sitting by the edge
of the pool in the forest. She waited a long time,
hoping the little boy would come again to take her
back to Fairyland to have another look at her children; but he did not; and though she came day after
day to the forest, and sat by the edge of the pool,
she never saw him again.

The three brothers often thought of their mother,
and wished to see her, but they were very happy
with the fairies who made ever so much of them.
They had been seven years in Fairyland, when Fairy
Prince got married, and there were great rejoicings
in the palace. There was a grand dinner to which
Dick, Jack, and Bill were invited, and after dinner a
grand ball, which was one of the finest things that
had ever been seen. The boys could not dance with
the fairies, who were of the small species, for fear
of treading upon them. They could only look on, and
after a while Dick and Jack got tired of it, and went
down to the garden to listen to the Queen's talking
bird, but Bill stayed in the ball-room to see the
bridegroom valse with the bride; for though Fairy

Prince looked such a handsome gentleman when he was up in the world, he was as little as the other fairies once he was below.

The talking bird perched on a tree at the end of the garden, and Tipsy watched every night at the foot of the tree lest any one should come and steal him. Dick and Jack now saw the dog there in the moonlight, but they also saw that he had dropped his silver bell, and that it lay in the grass beside him.

" That is Tipsy's silver bell," said Dick to Jack.

" Yes," answered the talking bird on the tree, " and if you take and tinkle it, you will find yourself in the place you came from; and you need only tinkle it whenever you wish to come back again to Fairyland."

When the boys heard this, they took each other by the hand. Dick picked up the little silver bell, and the moment it tinkled away they were out of Fairyland in the forest by the edge of the pool. Though it was night they made their way to their mother's house and knocked at the door, and when she heard their voices, she got up and let them in, and kissed them again and again, and cried for joy. Indeed she would have been quite happy now if it were not that

Bill had remained in Fairyland. Dick and Jack offered to go and look for him, but their mother was too much afraid of losing them again, and taking away the little silver bell, she hid it where they could not find it. Although Dick and Jack had been seven years away, they were no bigger, and looked no older than on the day when they ran away to the forest ; but each had learned his trade with the fairies, and could work beautifully. Dick made the prettiest little clothes, and Jack the prettiest little boots and shoes in the world, and though these things which they made were only fit for children, yet they had this advantage, that if the child who put them on were deformed, or a cripple, it became well at once. Their work was accordingly much sought after, and fetched so high a price that they earned a great deal of money and made their mother very happy and comfortable. There was only one drawback to all this : they remained little boys with round faces, rosy cheeks, and curly hair, whilst the boys whom they had known before they went to Fairyland, became young men, and got married, and had families of their own. The people who wanted them were always just as civil as if they had been big men with scrubby beards, but those who did not, jeered at and laughed at them till they were half sick of their lives, and wished themselves back again in Fairyland. Their mother, however, was just as kind to them as ever, and washed, and combed, and dressed them as if they had been little children still. She never seemed to understand that they ought to be grown-up men. She liked them as they were, and had only one trouble, that their brother Bill had not come back with them.

"Give us the little silver bell, mother," said Dick, "and let us all go off to Fairyland and find him."

But the widow said she was too old to go to Fairyland at her time of life, but that they might do as they pleased when she was dead. She lived for seven years after their coming back, and at the end of that time she died. Dick and Jack found the little silver bell round her neck and took it off. When she was buried they shut up the house and went to the forest. The moment they tinkled the bell they were off to Fairyland, and there they are to this day with their brother Bill working for the fairies.

K

The people who had laughed at them for remaining little boys were very sorry when they were gone, for no one ever made such pretty and useful little coats and shoes as theirs had been.

# Prince Doran.

ITTLE Prince Doran was seven years
with his nurse ; he was rocked seven years
more, and after that he slept seven years. Whilst
he was being rocked, his father the King gave him a
little black puppy-dog called Trim, and his mother the
Queen a little white kitten called Muff. Trim and
Muff were very fond of Doran, and slept with him, Muff
at his head, and Trim at his feet, until he awoke, and
then they woke too.

Prince Doran was now twenty-one, and as his father had died whilst he was sleeping, his mother the Queen said to him : " My dear, it is now time that you should get married. The Princess Sprightly is very beautiful and very rich ; you had better ask her to be your wife."

" I shall send an ambassador to ask her in marriage from the King her father," said Doran. And he did send the ambassador at once.

When Prince Doran was alone with Muff and Trim, and told them what he had done, Muff said, " The Princess lives a long way off ; she will be a long time coming. Why should we not go and see the world in the meantime ? "

" Muff," said Prince Doran, " you are the wisest cat I know."

And he went and told his mother that he, Muff, and Trim, were going to travel, and that they would all be back by the time the Princess arrived.

" My dear son," said the Queen, " you cannot leave your kingdom. You must stay and govern your subjects."

" Very well," answered Doran, " I shall stay."

That night Prince Doran told Muff and Trim, who

always slept with him, that he had agreed to remain at home, in order to govern his subjects. They were both very angry, and Trim said, " Why should not your cousin the Duke rule your kingdom whilst you are away ? And as to your subjects, they got on without you whilst you were sleeping ; can't they get on without you whilst you are travelling ? "

" I declare, Trim," cried Prince Doran, " you are a wonderful dog, and quite as wise as Muff."

When Doran told the Queen that he must go and travel all the same, and that his cousin the Duke would govern the kingdom in his stead, the Queen, who was very wise, shook her head and said, " My son, that will not do. Remember how long you have been sleeping, and how much time you have lost."

" Just so," answered Prince Doran, "I have slept so long that I mean to be wide awake now, and I also mean to make up for the time I have lost by going about."

All the Queen could say could not keep Prince Doran, his mind was so bent on travelling. So off he set with Muff and Trim, and all he took with him was a quilt, which he strapped to his knapsack. When

Muff was tired, Prince Doran carried him on his shoulder; when Trim was tired, Prince Doran carried him in his arms; and when Prince Doran himself was tired, he rolled himself up in his quilt, with Muff at his head and Trim at his feet, and the three had a long nap.

Prince Doran had been gone a long time, and he had already seen a great many wonderful things, when his mother, the Queen, sent him a messenger, who came all breathless with haste, to tell him that the Princess Sprightly had arrived, that she was the most beautiful Princess that had ever been seen, that she had brought with her forty chariots full of gold and precious stones, and that Prince Doran had better come back at once and marry her.

"You can't go home yet," said Muff, who was just then sitting on his shoulder, and who had heard every word the messenger had said; "you know you have not seen the great battle which is to take place between the cats and mice next month. How can you ever fight your enemies if you do not first see fighting?"

"I am glad you have thought of that, Muff," said

the Prince; "I must see the battle of course before I go home. Tell the Queen so," said he to the messenger; "but that as soon as Muff, Trim, and I have seen a little fighting, I shall make haste home, and marry the Princess."

The messenger went back to the Queen, and Prince Doran went on; but he was not in time to see the battle between the cats and mice, for it was just over when they arrived, and the cats, who had won the day, were burying their dead and eating their enemies. The Prince being too late for this, was thinking of going home in earnest, when the Queen sent him another messenger, telling him that the Princess Sprightly had been so much affronted at his thinking more of seeing a battle fought between cats and mice than of coming back to marry her; that she had talked of going away at once with her forty chariots. Whereupon his cousin the Duke, in order to avoid a war with the King her father, and also not to let all her valuables leave the kingdom, had married her.

"Well, that is settled," said Prince Doran; "what shall we do now?"

" Let us go and hear the wonderful bird who sings only once in a hundred years," said Trim.

" Yes," said Doran ; " we can go home after that."

The wonderful bird lived a long way off, and when they came to the country in which he was to be found, it wanted a good bit yet to the hundred years.

" Since we have come so far," said Prince Doran, " we shall wait till it is time for the wonderful bird to sing."

The Queen now sent another message to Doran. His subjects had got tired of waiting for him, and they had asked his cousin the Duke, who had consented, to be King in Prince Doran's stead. So upon the whole the Queen thought that Doran had better not come back.

" What can't be cured must be endured," said Doran ; " at least we shall hear the wonderful bird ; but let us take a nap till the hundred years are out."

He rolled himself up in his quilt, with Muff at his head and Trim at his feet, and the three went to sleep under a tree in a forest. They slept so soundly, and they slept so long, that, when they woke up, the wonderful bird, who perched on the tallest oak in the forest, had sung his song, and would not sing now for another hundred years.

" And now what shall we do ? " asked Doran.

" I think," answered Muff and Trim, " that we may just stay where we are."

" Then I must build a house," said Doran.

" Build it in the forest," said Trim ; " I want to go hunting."

" And leave plenty of room for the mice to run about," said Muff ; " a house without mice is dull."

Prince Doran did as they advised him. He built a house in the forest, and Muff and Trim helped him. When the house was built, and all but roofed, Doran, Muff, and Trim felt tired, and took a long nap.

" Let us roof the house now," said Doran, when he woke.

" No," said Trim, " let us hunt first."

" Yes, I want an airing," said Muff.

" Well," said Doran, " I feel as if a walk would do me good."

They all went out in the forest. Trim ran first looking for game, Doran came after him, and Muff was on Doran's shoulder. They had not walked long before Trim said, "I hear a great noise. Do you see anything, Muff?"

"I see two crows picking at something on the ground," answered Muff.

"Trim, go and see what is the matter," said Doran.

Trim went on barking till he came to the two crows. They flew away, and he found a little red squirrel all torn and bleeding, which he picked up in his mouth, and brought back to his master. The little Squirrel looked almost dead, but Prince Doran took it home and laid it on the hearth, and Trim licked it, and Muff kept it warm.

After a while the little Squirrel opened one eye, then he opened the other eye, then he moaned and stirred; then he said:

"Thank you, Prince Doran, you have saved my life."

Doran was accustomed to hear Muff and Trim talk but he had never heard a squirrel talk before; besides, this one knew his name, and could not be a squirrel like any other. He was much surprised, and said at once, "Who are you?"

"I am the Fairy Nap," answered the Squirrel; "and I am nurse to all the young fairies. I lull them to sleep by setting in motion all the gold and silver acorns on the fairy oak. I wanted to see the world, but the Queen of the Fairies would not allow it. I teased her so much, however, that she consented to let me have my way, but on condition that I should not be more than a week away, and that I should remain under the shape of a squirrel all the time. You see what has come of it. I had scarcely begun to look about me when I was attacked by these two crows, and they would have killed me if you had not sent Trim to deliver me."

Prince Doran, Muff, and Trim were greatly pleased to have got a fairy. They took every care of her, and they would sit and listen by the hour to her accounts of Fairyland. At the end of three days the Squirrel, or rather Fairy Nap, was quite well again, for she had told Doran to fetch her certain herbs from the forest, and these had healed her wounds. She was a little lame, however, for her left leg had been injured, but otherwise she was very lively, and ate the nuts which Muff and Trim brought her, as heartily as if she had eaten nothing else all her life. She would not sleep with Muff and Trim, however, but when Prince Doran took off his coat at night and hung it up, she got into his pocket and stayed there till the morning. The first thing he did on getting up was to look for Nap and take her out; but on the morning of the fourth day she was not in his pocket as usual.

"You need not look for me there, Prince Doran," said she, "I could not fit in your pocket now."

Doran looked round and saw the most beautiful little lady he had ever seen; and she was not merely beautiful, but she shone so with gold and silver and pearls, diamonds and precious stones, that he was quite dazzled.

"Are you Nap?" he asked.

"Yes," said she, "I am the Fairy Nap, and I must go back directly to Fairyland and lull the young fairies to sleep; and now tell me what gift you will have from me for having saved my life. But please to make haste, for I must be gone."

Prince Doran said he must consult Muff and Trim, so the three put their heads together and whispered to each other; then Prince Doran said, "Well, Nap, since you leave us free to choose, and since you are going back to Fairyland, take us with you."

Fairy Nap was very much vexed when she heard

this, and did all she could to make them change that
gift into another. She offered Doran to make him
king again, and Muff to give him a charm which
would make rats and mice run up to him, and Trim
to take him to Rabbitland, but they all three declared
that they would go to Fairyland, and that they would
have nothing else. When Nap saw they were deter-
mined, she thought she would make use of this wish of
theirs to see a little more of the world, but this time
under her own shape.

"Very well," said she; "if I take you to Fairyland,
you must lull the young fairies to sleep instead of me
for a week, and when you have been seven times seven
days in Fairyland you will find yourselves here back
again."

Prince Doran, Muff, and Trim agreed to this, for
they did not know that a week in Fairyland is exactly
seven times seven days, and not a minute less. The
moment they had said yes, they found themselves with
Nap in Fairyland under an oak-tree all hung with gold
and silver acorns. All the young fairies were lying
around the tree, and each fairy was in a cradle of
pearls, and from every gold and silver acorn there was

a thread, and all the threads met at one end and were fastened together by a big diamond. Nap put the diamond into Prince Doran's hand, and showed him how he was to put all the threads in motion, and lull the young fairies to sleep with the music of the gold and silver acorns ; then bidding him on no account stop one second, for if he did the young fairies would waken at once, and the Queen be ever so angry, she vanished. Prince Doran did as he was bid.  He set all the gold and silver acorns in motion, and lulled the young fairies to sleep ; but the music of the acorns was so sweet and delightful that he longed to sleep too ; so after a while he said, " Muff, take that ball in your mouth, and let me have a nod."

Muff did as he was bid ; but after a while he got so sleepy that he said, " Trim, take that ball in your mouth, and let me have a nod."

Trim took the ball, but he got so sleepy that he had to waken Prince Doran ; and when he got sleepy again, he had to waken Muff, and so they spent all their time sleeping and wakening ; and whilst Fairy Nap was going about the world enjoying herself, they could not stir from under the fairy tree, and never got a sight of

"Nap showed him how he was to put all the threads in motion, and lull the young fairies to sleep with the music of the gold and silver acorns."—*Page* 158.

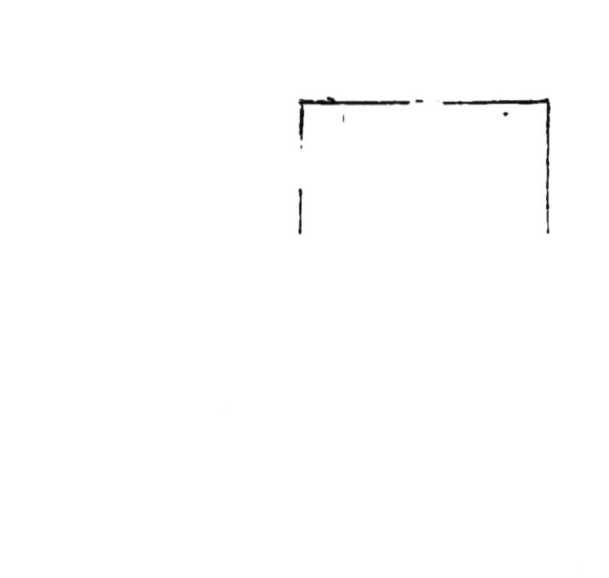

Fairyland. At last Doran got so tired that when he gave the ball to Muff he said, "Now, Muff, manage as you like ; but whatever you do, do not waken me."

"Very well," said Muff, as Prince Doran rolled himself up in his quilt and went fast asleep.

When Muff felt sleepy he gave the diamond ball to Trim, and said to him, "Now, Trim, manage as you like, but whatever you do, do not waken me."

With that Muff went and laid himself down at the head of Prince Doran, and was soon fast asleep.

Trim put the gold and silver acorns in motion, and lulled the young fairies to sleep as long as he could ; but he got so sleepy himself that he could go on no longer, so he just dropped the diamond ball, and curled himself round at the feet of Prince Doran.

The moment the diamond ball touched the ground the gold and silver acorns ceased going, and all the young fairies woke and began to cry. Trim started up, and picked up that nearest to him, and shook it well, he was so frightened. Then Muff awoke and got another fairy, and shook it too, to keep it quiet ; but as all the other fairies kept on crying louder and louder, Prince Doran awoke, and putting his hand in the cradle next him, he took the young fairy out of it and hushed it ; and at that moment the seven times seven days that they had been in Fairyland being out, Prince Doran, Muff, and Trim found themselves at home again in the little house in the forest ; Doran with a young fairy in his hand, and Muff and Trim with each a fairy in his mouth.

"Well," said Prince Doran, "we have brought something out of Fairyland."

They were all three much pleased with their prize. The young fairies were very little, but very pretty ; they required, however, so much care and nursing that Doran, Muff, and Trim had no time to spare to roof the house, for Doran made cradles for them, and they had to be rocked almost all day and all night ; then they could feed on nothing but dew and honey, and Doran had to go out every morning to get them the earliest dew, and Muff had to prowl about at night to steal the honey of the wild bees for them, whilst Trim stayed at home and watched them, and would not let a soul come near the place. All that time the house remained unroofed ; but on account of there being fairies in it, there was neither rain nor bad weather.

It was always sunny in the daytime and warm at night. When the young fairies were old enough to go about they were so frolicsome and so full of pretty tricks that Doran, Muff, and Trim never felt dull, and grew fonder and fonder of them every day. Indeed they could not let them out of their sight a moment lest they should escape. Not that the young fairies seemed to wish to go ; but Doran knew that fairies are not to be trusted, besides he was afraid lest the Queen of the Fairies should steal these back again from him, Muff, and Trim.

One day Doran's fairy said to him, "Doran, you must open all the doors and windows of the house."

"Why so?" asked Doran.

" Because we are going to make you, Muff, and Trim a quilt to lie on, and we want all the birds of the air, all the fishes of the sea, and all the insects of the field to help us."

When Muff and Trim saw Doran opening all the doors and windows of the house, they asked him what that was for, and when Doran told them, Trim said : "Your old quilt would do very well. What do you want with a new one?"

L

And Muff said: " I would not trust those fairies, if I were you."

But for once Doran would not take the advice of Muff and Trim. When all the doors and windows of the house were open, the first fairy called all the birds of the air, and made each bird give her a feather; then the second fairy called all the fishes of the sea, and bade each fish give her a scale or bring her a pearl from the sea ; then the third fairy called all the insects of the field, and made every one of those that spun webs give her some of their web, and those that were winged one of its wings. When they had all the feathers, scales, pearls, wings, and webs that they wanted, the young fairies began to make the quilt. They worked three days and three nights, and at length the quilt was finished. The groundwork was of feathers and web to be soft and warm, the pattern was of fishes' scales and insects' wings, and the border and the tassels were of pearls.

"And now," said the fairies to Doran, " lie down and try if you like your quilt."

Doran lay down, and the quilt was so soft and warm and pleasant, that he rolled himself in it and fell asleep at once.

" And now, Muff," said the fairies, " try how you like the quilt."

Muff went and laid himself down at Doran's head and fell fast asleep.

" And now," said the fairies to Trim, " do you try how you like it, Trim."

Trim crept under the quilt till he got at Doran's feet, when he at once began to snore. When the three were fast asleep, the fairies went and sat on the quilt. Then it rose and rose till it flew away up in the air, because there was no roof to the house, and Doran, Muff, and Trim and the three fairies were in Fairyland in no time, all under the oak-tree with the gold and silver acorns, where Nap was lulling the young fairies to sleep in their cradles of pearls. When Doran, Muff, and Trim had had a long sleep they awoke.

" Why, here we are, under the oak-tree again," said Doran.

" Yes," said the three young fairies, " and here we are with you, and is not that a good quilt which we made for you ? "

" It is very good," answered Prince Doran, " but I am tired hearing the gold and silver acorns, besides I must go home and roof my house."

" Have another sleep first," said the three fairies.

" Yes," said Muff and Trim, " let us take another nap."

So they all three went to sleep again, and the three young fairies watched by them night and day lest they should escape, and every time they woke and wanted to go home, they persuaded them to have another sleep first, and that is how Doran, Muff, and Trim are still asleep in Fairyland, and how the little house in the forest is unroofed to this day.

# Fairie and Brownie.

**T**HERE was once upon a time, a poor old woman, who lived in a little cottage on the borders of a forest, with her two orphan grandchildren. They were twin sisters, and so much alike that their grandmother only knew them by the colour of their hair; for one was fair and the other was dark, and the fair one was called Fairie, and the dark one, Brownie.

The old woman went out one day to gather sticks in the forest, and left the two children alone in the

house. It was a Saturday, and Fairie, who was looking out of the window to see the people who went
up and down the road, on their way to and from
market, also began to sing.

"Ding, dong, dell,"

sang Fairie, and Brownie answered within,

"Pussy cat's in the well."
"Who put him in?"

sang Fairie.

"Little Johnnie Trim,"

answered Brownie.

"Who took him out?"

Fairie sang again and again.  Brownie answered,

"Little Johnnie Trout."

The two sisters were beginning again with "Ding,
dong, dell," when a little old gentleman turned round
the corner of the house and looked up at Fairie.  He
wore a cocked hat, a red coat, silk stockings, and
shoes with silver buckles to them, for all this happened
a long time ago, when people were still dressed after
that fashion.

"My dear," said the old gentleman, winking at

Fairie, "how well you do sing. Will you let me in to listen to your 'Ding, dong, dell'?"

"The door is on the latch, sir," replied Fairie, "and you can come in if you like."

"Oh! very well," says he briskly, and in he walked at once.

Fairie, who was never afraid of anything, or of any one, came and looked at him; but Brownie, who was shy, ran and hid behind the door. The old gentleman took a chair, sat down, and made himself comfortable. Presently he took off his cocked hat, and said to Fairie: "My dear, your 'Ding, dong, dell' is the prettiest and the cleverest song I ever heard. Do sing it to me, please. In my right ear, dear."

"Yes," answered Fairie; "but Brownie must sing, 'Pussy cat's in the well.'"

"By all means," said he; "Brownie shall sing in my left ear."

Fairie began at once with "Ding, dong, dell," which she sang in the old gentleman's right ear, and Brownie sang "Pussy cat's in the well" in his left ear, and they both sang till the song was ended, when they began it again, for as the old gentleman said : One can never have too much of a good thing.   Indeed, so nicely did they sing, and so pleased was he, that he shut his eyes and purred like a cat.   They had just begun another "Ding, dong, dell," when the door opened, and their grandmother came in with her bundle of sticks.

"There, dears, that will do, thank you," said the old gentleman, getting up and walking out.

Something fell on the floor with a chink as he got up, and Fairie ran after him, saying: "You have dropped something, sir."

"Keep it, my dear," answered the old gentleman without looking round.

He walked on very fast, got behind some tall ferns, and vanished.   When Fairie went back to the cottage and told her grandmother all that had happened, she found that it was a bright new shilling which the old gentleman had dropped on the floor.   People could live for a week on a shilling in those times ; and as the old grandmother was very poor, she thought what a blessing it was that this gentleman in the cocked hat should have come in and got Fairie and Brownie to sing him "Ding, dong, dell."

On the following Saturday the grandmother went out again to the forest to gather sticks, and the two little sisters remained at home. Fairie was at the window, looking up and down the road, when she saw the old gentleman in the red coat and cocked hat coming towards the house.

"Well, my dear," said he, nodding to her, "will you let me in to-day?"

"Oh yes, sir," answered Fairie; "and we will sing you 'Four-and-twenty blackbirds baked in a pie,' if you like it."

"Thank you, dear," said he, walking in; "but I think 'Ding, dong, dell,' the finest song that ever was made, and we will have that first, if you please."

He sat down, took off his cocked hat, made Fairie sing in his right ear and Brownie in his left; and when the song was ended, and they wanted to have the "Four-and-twenty blackbirds baked in a pie," he begged for "Ding, dong, dell" over again, for, as he said, the more he heard that noble song the better he liked it. They were beginning it for the seventh time when the door opened, and their grandmother came in with a bundle of sticks in her arm. The old gentleman then started up in a mighty hurry, and dropped another shilling as he walked out of the house.   Brownie picked it up and ran after him, but he did not even look round at her.

"Keep it, keep it," said he; and he was gone and behind the ferns in no time.

Well, this shilling lasted another week; and when Saturday came round, the grandmother went again to the forest to gather sticks, and the old gentleman came and had "Ding, dong, dell" sung to him by the two little sisters; and everything happened exactly as it had happened before, with this difference, that it was the grandmother who ran after him with the shilling, and that, being rather lame, she was only just in time to see his cocked hat disappear behind the ferns. She went on thinking she would surely find him; but when she, too, got behind the ferns, all she saw was a molehill.

"Now, who can this little gentleman in the red coat be, and where does he come from, and where does he go to?" thought the grandmother. "I shall stay within next Saturday and watch him."

Instead of going out to gather sticks as usual, the

old woman remained at home on the next Saturday; but though both Fairie and Brownie had their heads out of the window, and sang "Ding, dong, dell," and looked up and down the road for the old gentleman, he never came near the cottage. The grandmother got tired of waiting for him, and went out towards dusk. She was scarcely gone when in he walked, looking in a great hurry.

"Come, my dears," said he to the children, "make haste and sing, for I am ever so late."

Fairie and Brownie, who were very good-natured, began singing at once; but at the end of five minutes he started up and said that would do for to-day, and he had dropped the shilling, and was gone in a moment.

Matters went on so for a long time. The grandmother, seeing it was no use to stay at home and watch the old gentleman, went out every Saturday. He came quite regularly to hear "Ding, dong, dell" sung, and dropped a shilling, as a matter of course, and walked away and vanished behind the ferns just as he had done the first time. One Saturday, as the old grandmother was coming in and the old gentleman was going out, he said to Fairie and Brownie: "Well, dears, I shall come and hear 'Ding, dong, dell' sung for the last time next Saturday, and so what shall I bring you?"

Before the grandmother had time to put in a word, both Fairie and Brownie had answered: "Oh, please, will you bring us a bird?"

"Very well," said he, "you shall have 'Don't-Forget-Me.'" And off he was, and behind the ferns in no time. The grandmother was very angry that Fairie and Brownie had asked for nothing better than a bird.

"You foolish children," she said, "what shall we do with a bird? Feed it when we cannot feed ourselves! And then, how shall we get on without the old gentleman's shilling since he means to come no more? If you had sung something else to him besides that stupid 'Ding, dong, dell,' he would never have left off coming, I am sure."

She scolded them both till Fairie and Brownie began to cry, and declared that they had sung "Ding, dong, dell" because the old gentleman would hear nothing else, and he shut his eyes and purred all the time they sang it, and they were sure they were not to blame.

"Well," said the grandmother, "what is done is done, but what you have to do is this: when that little Red Coat goes away next Saturday, follow him as fast as you can, and see where he goes to when he gets behind the ferns. If you can find out where he lives, he may take you to sing to him again."

Fairie and Brownie both promised to do this. The old gentleman came on the Saturday, and they sang to him, and as he was going away, he took a little silver cage with a green bird in it out of his pocket, and said: "Good-bye, my dears, here is 'Don't-Forget-Me.'" And he was gone in no time. Fairie and Brownie followed him out, and as he never looked round, they were almost as soon behind the ferns as he was. They saw him walking very fast to a broad and handsome gate which stood wide open, showing them a beautiful garden full of roses, and beyond it a splendid palace all glittering in the sun. "I suppose he lives here," said Fairie to Brownie; and they followed him in. No sooner had they passed the gate than the old gentleman looked round and nodded to them. "Oh! Fairie and Brownie," said he, "here you are come to see me! I thought you would.

Well, my dears, your room is ready, and luncheon is waiting."

He took them at once to the palace, then up to a pretty room with two little beds in it. And on each bed there was a pretty little frock ready ; the blue one was for Fairie, and Brownie had the pink one. After that they went to another room where a table was set out with cakes, sweets, and all sorts of good things. The old gentleman bade the little sisters take what they liked and eat as much as they pleased. When they had done he made them sing to him, and after that he took them to a room full of playthings, where he left them.

Now this old gentleman was prime minister to the King of the Fairies, and his name was Snip. The beautiful palace he had taken Fairie and Brownie to was the palace of the King and Queen, and it was in Fairyland. There was nothing Snip liked so well as hearing little children sing, and he went out in the world every Saturday for that purpose, till the King, who wanted him for state business, would not let him out any more. You may think, therefore, how glad Snip was to keep Fairie and Brownie when they followed him. He was very kind to them, and gave them the best of everything. They had all sorts of dainty things to eat, and the most beautiful clothes to wear, and the handsomest of playthings. to play with, and all they had to do was to sing " Ding, dong, dell" to him every day. Sometimes they got tired of this, and cried, and asked to go home to Granny ; but Snip gave them a cake or a doll or a new frock, and they were comforted.

No one in the palace knew anything about all this, but the King and Queen of the Fairies soon perceived that the prime minister who dined at the royal table, was always in a great hurry to go to his own apartment immediately after luncheon.

"Snip," once said the King, "what are you going away for in such haste ? "

" May it please your Majesty," answered Snip, look-ing mysterious. " I know that your Majesty's enemies are plotting against you, so I go and counterplot in my room."

The King nodded, and said, " Quite right," and that was all.

The King had a little fairy page called Pop, who was

always making mischief. As he once passed by the door of Snip he heard him talking to Fairy and Brownie. Pop was too short to look through the keyhole and see who was within, but he ran and told the King that the prime minister had strangers with him.

"Snip is a traitor," said the King to the Queen, "I must see about it."

The King went at once to the door of Snip's room, and wishing to take the prime minister in the act, whatever he might be doing, he first peeped through the keyhole. What should he see but Snip seated in an armchair, with his eyes shut, and his hands folded, a little fair girl standing on one side of him, and a little dark girl on the other.

"Now, my dears, you may begin," said Snip.

" Ding, dong, dell," sang Fairie in his right ear.

"Pussy cat's in the well," sang Brownie in his left ear, and so on, till the song was ended, and all the time Snip kept his eyes shut, and purred like a cat.

They were going to begin over again, when the King touched the lock with the fairy ring on his fore finger. At once the door flew wide open, Snip started up in a fright, and Fairie and Brownie went and hid behind his big chair.

"Well, sir," said the King of the Fairies, looking very sternly at Snip, and speaking in a very deep voice, "is that your counterplotting, having 'Ding, dong, dell,' sung to you by two mortals? Don't you know that I have forbidden all such intercourse with human beings since we had so much trouble with Red Cap?"

"May it please your Majesty," replied Snip, who was himself again, "I do it to clear my ideas, and for the good of your kingdom. Your Majesty knows that we fairies get cobweb on the brain. Now, to hear a song sung by human beings, who, as every one knows, never have cobwebs of any kind, is the finest thing in the world for that complaint. Your Majesty cannot imagine how clear one's ideas begin to get when one hears 'Ding, dong, dell,' but when it comes to Johnny Trout, one feels as bright as bright can be."

"Indeed!" said the King, "I must try that. Give me the chair, and you little things come and sing to me directly."

It took some coaxing to make Fairie and Brownie

M

sing to the King of the Fairies, but at length they did so, and he liked it amazingly.

"I declare my ideas are getting clearer and clearer," said the King, "I must hear that wonderful song every day. 'Ding, dong, dell!' Beautiful! beautiful!"

"And Pussy cat's in the well!" said Snip.

"Oh! that is fine," said the King:

"And Johnny Trout!" said Snip.

"Oh! that beats all," said the King, "but, Snip, we will keep this to ourselves. We will not tell the Queen about it."

When he had heard "Ding, dong, dell," sung for ever so long, the King of the Fairies went and told the Queen that Pop was a little impostor, and that Snip was a great statesman.

"Well, but what about your enemies, and the plotting and counterplotting," said the Queen.

"My dear," answered the King, "these are state matters, with which ladies have nothing to do."

The Queen was very much affronted at this, and would not look at either Snip or the King for ever so long. After a time, however, she thought she would like to know what it was that kept them closeted together every day, and so one afternoon she went to Snip's door and listened to what was going on within. The King was scolding Snip, and talking so loud that the Queen could hear every word.

"I tell you, sir," he was saying, "it is my turn to hear 'Ding, dong, dell.' How dare you keep your sovereign waiting, you rebel?"

But Snip answered quite coolly, "May it please your Majesty, I brought Fairie and Brownie here, and though I may lend them to you, they are mine for all that."

"No, we are not," cried Fairie and Brownie; "we are Granny's, and we want to go away, and we will not sing any more for you, you bad, ugly little men."

Here was a fine thing! Two puny human beings calling the King of the Fairies and his prime minister bad, ugly little men!

"Snip, you are a traitor," cried the King in a rage. "You set these little creatures against me. Come here and sing to me directly," he said to Fairie.

"And you come and sing to me," said Snip to Brownie.

When the Queen heard about singing, she looked

through the keyhole. She saw the King sitting in a chair, Fairie singing to him, and he purring like a cat with his eyes shut, and Snip sitting in another chair with Brownie singing to him, and he was purring louder than the King. When the Queen had looked long enough she went away. Presently she met the King and his minister, who had made it up, and were going out riding together. She asked what they had been doing in Snip's room.

"My dear," answered the King, "I have already told you that these are state matters not fit for ladies."

"Oh, very well," said the Queen; but as soon as they were gone, she went up to Snip's room and touched the lock with the fairy ring on her forefinger. The door flew open, and the Queen found Fairie and Brownie crying together in a corner of the room.

They stopped when the Queen of the Fairies came in, for never before had they seen so beautiful a lady, and one so finely dressed too, all in gold and silver, with a crown of diamonds on her head.

"Who are you?" asked the Queen. "Who brought you here, and what are you crying for?"

"I am Fairie, and this is Brownie," answered Fairie,

" and we came here after an ugly little black man, because Granny bade us, and the ugly little black man makes us sing to him, and we want to go home to Granny."

"Very well," said the Queen; "but as you did not come here from naughtiness, but because you were bid, you must see my garden first."

She took Fairie by one hand and Brownie by the other, and went down to the garden with them. She then bade them bring her all the cobwebs they could find. They did so, and when she had cobwebs enough, the Queen took a needle out of a little housewife in her pocket, and bidding the sisters mind what she was doing, she began to work the cobwebs till they became the finest and most beautiful lace that had ever been seen.

"Now, take a cobweb, and do as I did," said the Queen, giving each a housewife like her own.

Fairie and Brownie did as the Queen told them, and each worked her cobweb till it was almost as beautiful as the Queen's.

"Now put up your housewife, and let us look at my garden," said the Queen.

They went over the garden, which was a most
beautiful place, and full of the loveliest roses and
rarest flowers. Fairie asked if Brownie and she might
not take some. The Queen at first said no, that she
never allowed any one to pick the flowers of her garden ; then she changed her mind, and told them that
as they had been good children she would let them
take a few. Fairie gathered some white roses, and
made a wreath of them, which she put on her head ;
and Brownie picked some crimson berries that grew
on a tree, and threaded them into a necklace, which
she fastened round her neck. This was scarcely done,
when Fairie saw the gate through which they had
come in standing wide open.

"Oh, please," said Fairie to the Queen, "may I
just run out to Granny? I see her there beyond,
gathering sticks in the forest."

"I have a hundred gardens, and you have seen
only one," answered the Queen. "Which will you see
first, your Granny or my other ninety-nine gardens?"

Fairie and Brownie both said they would rather
see their Granny first, upon which the Queen told them
to go. They ran out at once in the forest, ever so

glad to see their grandmother again, but also wishing much to see the other ninety-nine gardens of the Queen of the Fairies.

"We shall be back directly," said Fairie, turning round, but she stared quite amazed, for lo! the gate was gone, there was not a glimpse of the garden and its roses, the glittering palace had vanished, and they were alone in the forest, with the tall ferns around them, and not a sign of their grandmother far or near.

The two little sisters were so frightened, that Brownie could not help crying; but Fairie took her hand, and said she knew the way home, and that if Granny was out they could sit at the door and wait till she came back. They went round the ferns, and followed the highroad. They met several people, who all stared at Fairie's wreath of roses and at Brownie's necklace of berries, till the children were ashamed, and hid them in the pockets of their little pinafores, for all the fine things which Snip had given them were gone, and they wore the shabby clothes which they had on when they followed him. They came at last to the spot where their grandmother's cottage should have been, but in its stead they saw a big square

house, with four-and-twenty windows on every side,
and four-and-twenty weathercocks on the roof.

"Please, whose house is that?" asked Fairie of a
woman who was passing by.

"Why, you silly child," answered the woman, "where
do you come from that you do not know this is the
house which the Queen had built for Don't-Forget-
Me?"

The children were glad to hear about Don't-Forget-
Me, for they thought that perhaps their grandmother
lived there now. They went and sat on the door-
steps, and waited, thinking she might come out to
them, but she did not, and in her stead out walked
a big servant man in livery, who asked them roughly
what they were doing there.

"We are tired, and we are resting," said a little voice,
and Fairie, looking up, saw Don't-Forget-Me in his
silver cage, hanging out of a window.

"Then don't rest long," said the big servant man, as
he went back into the house.

Presently a lady's maid came out, and calling the
children little lazy things, bade them begone.

"We are not lazy, for we can make lace out of cobwebs," said the little voice again; "go and say so to your lady the Princess, and show her this."

Fairie, seeing what Don't-Forget-Me meant, took out of her pocket the lace which she had worked in the garden of the Queen of the Fairies, and gave it to the lady's maid, who went in with it to her mistress the Princess.

Now, this Princess was so fond of lace that she spent almost all her money upon it, though she could never find any to her liking ; but nothing could be finer than this lace made of cobweb, and it was so beautiful as well, that the Princess declared she had never seen anything to equal it.

" Bring those wonderful little girls at once," said she to the maid.

" Children," said she, when they stood before her, "did you really make this lace out of cobwebs ?"

" Get us some cobwebs from the garden and you will see," said a little voice.

Fairie and Brownie looked up, and there was Don't-Forget-Me in his silver cage, hanging close to them.

The Princess sent to the garden for some cobwebs.

She chose the finest, and gave them to Fairie and Brownie, who, each taking out her housewife, at once made the most beautiful lace that could be seen.

"And who taught you how to make lace out of cobweb, and who are you?" asked the Princess, more amazed than ever.

"A lady who lives far away taught us," answered Don't-Forget-Me in his cage; "and we are orphans."

"Will you stay with me and work lace for me?" asked the Princess.

"Oh yes; we will," answered Don't-Forget-Me, "if you will use us kindly."

The Princess, who never seemed to know it was Don't-Forget-Me who was talking, and not Fairie and Brownie, promised to be very kind to them; but she did not keep her word, for the first thing she did was to have them taken to a room at the top of the house, and locked up there, lest they should escape, and make lace out of cobwebs for some one else.

When Fairie and Brownie saw that they could not get out any more, they were in great trouble.

"Don't fret," said a little voice, "I shall keep you company."

They looked up and saw Don't-Forget-Me in his silver cage.

"Oh, Don't-Forget-Me," said Fairie, "when will Granny come to see us?"

"My dear," answered Don't-Forget-Me, "guess how long you have been away."

"Seven days," said Fairie, "for we left on the Saturday morning, and this is Friday."

"My dear," replied Don't-Forget-Me, "you have been gone seven years, and your grandmother is dead."

Fairie and Brownie cried bitterly on hearing this, but Don't-Forget-Me did his best to comfort them. He promised to stay with them and to advise them, and he also told them all that had happened whilst they were in Fairyland. When the old grandmother saw that Fairie and Brownie did not come back from the forest, she went to look for them behind the ferns, but neither there nor anywhere else did she find them. She came back alone to the cottage, and sitting down, she began to cry.

"Don't cry, Granny," said a little voice.

"Why, who are you?" asked the grandmother, looking around her and seeing no one.

"I am Don't-Forget-Me," answered the little voice, "and my silver cage is just behind you. I belong to Fairie and Brownie, and you must not fret, Granny, for they are well and happy, and are busy singing 'Ding, dong, dell' to the old gentleman this very minute, but they cannot come back for seven years."

"And what shall I do all that time?" asked the poor old woman.

"Don't be afraid, Granny," answered Don't-Forget-Me, "but take me to-morrow to the Queen."

Granny did as she was bid. She took Don't-Forget-Me in his silver cage to the palace, and asked to show him to the Queen. Before her Majesty could say a word, the young Prince, who was very rude, burst out laughing, and said: "You silly old woman, what does the Queen want with your bird? What can he do for her?"

"I can tell the Queen that you broke her fan yesterday," said Don't-Forget-Me.

The young Prince was quite frightened when he heard this little bird telling what he had done, but the Queen was both surprised and delighted.

"You wonderful bird," said she, "you must come and live in my palace, and talk to me every day."

But Don't-Forget-Me said he could not do that on any account; however, if the Queen would build him a house to his liking, with a few other things he should tell her of, he should not mind staying in it, and letting her come and talk to him every morning. The Queen agreed to everything, for with such a bird as Don't-Forget-Me to advise her, she knew she could do without her ministers, who were rather trouble-some about that time.

The first thing Don't-Forget-Me asked for was, that the Queen should build him a house with twenty-four windows on every side, and twenty-four weather-cocks on the roof, and that this house should be on the spot where the old grandmother's cottage stood. The next thing Don't-Forget-Me asked for was, a large garden, with trees and flowers; and last of all, that his Granny should take care of him, and have a set of servants under her, to keep everything nice, and in order. All this the Queen did very willingly; and every morning she went and had a long conversation with Don't-Forget-Me, who told her all she was to do, and who made quite a great queen of her.

When Don't-Forget-Me had been a year in his

new house, poor old Granny died, and he told the
Queen she must find him a Princess to take care of
him. The Queen had some trouble in getting him a
Princess to his liking, but she did find one at last
that suited him, and matters went on very comfort-
ably, till the Queen died too, and the young Prince
reigned in her stead. The new King would have nothing to say to Don't-Forget-Me, whom he hated, but
at the same time, he feared him too much to do anything against him. So Don't-Forget-Me lived in his
house with the Princess till Fairie and Brownie came
back from Fairyland.

The Princess was very much surprised to find that
instead of staying in the drawing-room with her, Don't-
Forget-Me would now be in the room at the top of
the house with the two little girls. He told her that
he wanted to see them making lace out of cobwebs,
and as after all he was the master of the house, there
was no gainsaying him. He was so kind to Fairie
and Brownie that they did not mind being locked up,
for Don't-Forget-Me told them the most beautiful
fairy tales, and he taught them ever so many things
as well, and the two sisters were as happy as the day

was long, till they grew up to be beautiful young women. All these years they spent in making lace out of cobwebs, till there was scarcely a cobweb to be found in field or garden, and spiders had to be reared like silkworms. Their lace was the finest and the rarest to be seen, and the Princess was as proud as could be of the handsome things she had ; but she had nothing so handsome as the robe and veil which each of the sisters made for her own wedding-day, by the advice of Don't-Forget-Me.

"But, Don't-Forget-Me," once said Fairie, "who will ever come up here to marry us ?"

"Some one will come by and by," answered Don't-Forget-Me ; "do as I bid you."

The Princess had two sons, who had gone off travelling to see the world the very day before that on which Fairie and Brownie left Fairyland. These two young Princes had many strange adventures, and saw many wonderful things, but they had never seen anything more wonderful than Don't-Forget-Me, and when they came back, the first thing they asked of their mother was : "Where is Don't-Forget-Me ?"

"He is busy," answered the Princess, "you cannot

see him to-day; besides he does not like company any longer."

The Princes were sorry to hear this, for Don't-Forget-Me had been very kind to them formerly, and he had told them all about Fairie and Brownie, and how they were to come back from Fairyland when their seven years were out.

"I shall marry Fairie," had said the elder one of the two Princes, "I like her best."

"And I shall marry Brownie," said his brother, "I like her best."

"Very well," said Don't Forget-Me; "but you must go and travel first, and by the time you are home again, Fairie and Brownie will be here."

The young Princes did as Don't-Forget-Me bade them, and when they came back, and were told they could not see him, the next question they put was: "Have not Fairie and Brownie left Fairyland yet?"

But their mother did not even know what they meant, for she had never heard of Fairie and Brownie. The Princes had been home three days, and they were wondering to each other in what part of the house Don't-Forget-Me was to be found, when, as they were walking in the garden, they heard him talking to Fairie and Brownie, who had left the window of their room open.

"Oh! Don't-Forget-Me, where are you?" cried the Princes from below.

"Come up to the top of the house," he answered in his little clear voice, which could be heard ever so far, "and open the first door you see, and you will find me there."

The Princes did as Don't-Forget-Me told them; they went up to the top of the house, and opened the first door they saw; for, though the Princess had locked the door, she had forgotten to take the key. When the Princes entered the room, they looked for Don't-Forget-Me; but, instead of him, they saw two beautiful girls, one fair and one dark, who were making lace out of cobwebs. At first they were both so much amazed that they could not say one word, but at length the elder one of the two Princes, looking at Fairie, said: "Who are you, and where do you come from?"

"I am Fairie," she answered; "that is my sister Brownie, and we come from Fairyland."

N

"Then if you are Fairie," said the Prince, "Don't-Forget-Me has surely told you that you are to marry me, and that Brownie is to marry my brother there."

"Yes," said Don't-Forget-Me, in his cage; "I have told them all that, and their wedding-dresses are ready, but you must go and ask the Princess for her consent."

The Princes lost no time in going to their mother, and telling her that they had found Fairie and Brownie, and wished to marry them.

"Very well," said the Princess; "but if you do marry them, I must have Don't-Forget-Me."

When the Princes went back and told Fairie and Brownie this, the two sisters cried out that they liked the Princes very much, but that they could never part with Don't-Forget-Me, who had been so good to them all these years.

"Do as I bid you," said Don't-Forget-Me, who had been listening to all this, "and tell the Princess that you will not give me up till you are married; and that then you must open my cage, take me out and stroke me three times, and kiss me twice, before you put me on her hand."

"'Now I have you,' said she."—*Page* 195.

Fa·rie and Brownie, who knew how wise Don't-Forget-Me was, did as he bade them; and the Princess was so glad to get this wonderful bird, that she made her sons marry the two sisters the very next morning. Fairie and Brownie put on their beautiful lace robes and veils, and Fairie's wreath of roses, which she had kept all these years, turned out to be diamonds, and Brownie's necklace of berries to be rubies; and the two brides looked so beautiful and so good, that every one said how happy the Princess ought to be to have got such wives for her sons.

The Princess said she was very glad; but, to say the truth, it was because she was to get Don't-Forget-Me that she was so pleased. She asked for him as soon as the wedding was over. The cage was brought down to the drawing-room; and when the Princess had ordered all the doors and windows to be shut, Fairie and Brownie opened the cage and took out Don't-Forget-Me. Each stroked him three times and kissed him twice, then both put him on the Princess' hand.

"Now I have you," said she. But even as she spoke all the doors and windows flew wide open.

"Good-bye," said Don't-Forget-Me ; and off and away he flew to Fairyland, where he has remained ever since, and all that the Princess had of him was his silver cage. She was in great trouble at first, but Fairie and Brownie comforted her, and were very good and kind ; and they were all very happy together till they died.

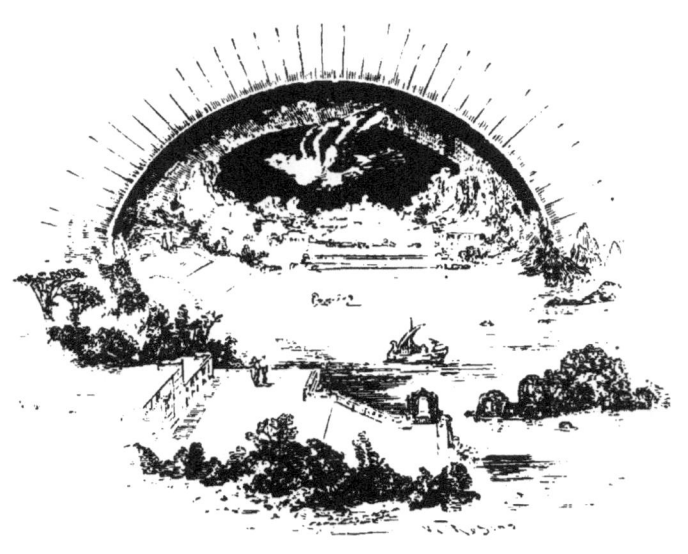

# Batty.

WERE three Princesses once
who were very beautiful and very

proud. Each Princess built herself a palace with a
turret to it. When the turrets were nearly finished,
the Princesses having heard of the three silver bells of
Fairyland, wished to have them to roof their turrets
with. They sent out a proclamation, offering to marry
the kings who would get the bells for them. No kings,
however, caring to make the attempt, the Princesses
said they would take up with princes. When this,
too, failed, they sent out a third proclamation, saying
they would marry the men who brought them the
bells, no matter who and what they might be. Upon
this, a great many young men set off for Fairyland, and
tried to get in, and bring back the bells, in order to
marry the Princesses; but they all failed, no doubt, for
not one of them ever appeared again. So the Princesses
remained unmarried, and the turrets unroofed, and all
on account of the three silver bells of Fairyland.

Well, about this very same time there lived a poor
Woodcutter and his wife, who had three sons. The first
was big Billy, the second was bigger Billy, and the third
was biggest Billy. When the first Billy was born, the
Woodcutter said: "What a fine child." When the
second Billy came, the Woodcutter said: "That child is

very large ;" but when he saw the third Billy, the poor Woodcutter cried out: " This is a Giant ! How shall I ever feed him and his brothers ?" Indeed the three boys grew up so tall, so stout, and so large, that every one called them the Giants ; and they were as awkward and as ungainly as they were big. They were good for nothing, said their father, but to mar his work, fill the place, and eat him out of house and home. There were a great many bats in the old tower, and looking at them, the Woodcutter used to say : "I would rather have a bat for a child than another Billy."

The tower stood on the borders of a forest, which was close to Fairyland. The fairies thought they would give the Woodcutter his wish, and the next child his wife had, instead of being a girl, was the prettiest little bat in the world. The Woodcutter was very angry at first, but his wife said to him : "I wonder at you. Bats are dear little things to begin with, and this is the dearest little bat I ever saw. Besides, you will see how nice it will look when I have dressed it."

The Woodcutter's wife made her little bat a pair of red mittens and a pair of red stockings, and when she had them on, she looked so well and so pretty in them, that her father began to like her. The Giants, too, were very fond of Batty, and helped to nurse her until she was strong enough to fly. She, too, was very fond of them, and would hang from them when she wanted a nod in the daytime, or wheel about their heads of an evening; but after all, there was nothing she liked so well as sleeping in the old tower all day, and flitting about it at night. She got on very well with the other bats, for though they were all much older than she was, they thought a great deal of her on account of her red mittens.

The Woodcutter liked Batty, chiefly because she gave him no trouble, and cost him nothing, but the three poor Billies he hated more and more.

"They are good for nothing, but to sleep, eat, and drink," he would say. "If they had any spirit, they would never stay here. If they can do nothing else, can't they go for the three silver bells of Fairyland?"

"But if they do, I shall never see them again," said the Woodcutter's wife, crying.

Batty, who was hanging by her heels in a dark corner of the room, heard all this, and wondered what it meant.

"Mother," said she, as soon as her father was out, "what are the three silver bells of Fairyland, and why does father want my brothers to go for them?"

Her mother then told her the story of the three Princesses who had offered to marry the young men who would bring them back the bells with which they wished to roof their turrets. "But if my Billies go to Fairyland," said the Woodcutter's wife, "I know I shall never see them again."

"Do not fret, mother," said Batty; "if my brothers go to Fairyland, I shall go with them, and bring them safe home."

This comforted the Woodcutter's wife a little, for she knew that Batty was very clever, and could take good care of the Giants. Batty went at once to an old bat who lived in the tower, and asked her how she was to go to Fairyland.

"It is the easiest thing in the world," answered the old bat; "wait till the moon is up, get on a moonbeam, and it will take you straight to Fairyland."

Batty did as the old bat told her. She waited till the moon was up, got on a moonbeam, and soon found herself in Fairyland, close to the King's palace. She saw the three silver bells in a belfry, shining in the moonlight, and she was flitting about them, when the fairy, whose business it was to watch the bells, cried out : "Who goes there ?"

"Little Batty," said she.

"What brings you here ?"

"I came to see the silver bells."

"That's all very well," said the fairy, "but the King must have a look at you."

He took Batty before the King and the Queen of the Fairies, who, as soon as they saw her, cried out, "Why, that is little Batty. We know her by her red mittens. Well, Batty, so you have come to see Fairyland ; and what do you think of it ?"

"I think I never saw so fine a place," said Batty; "but may it please your Majesties to tell me what is the use of these silver bells up in the belfry ?"

"These bells," said the King, " are to waken us in the morning ; to call us to dinner at noon ; and to send us to sleep at night. Would you like the Queen to let you have a look at them, Batty ?"

Batty answered that she would very much like to see the bells, so the Queen took her up to the belfry, showed her the bells, and then said, " I think you had better go now, Batty. We like you very well, but we want no strangers here. Come, get up on the moonbeam and be off."

Batty got up on the moonbeam, and she was at home in the old tower long before day. No one asked her where she had been, and Batty said nothing about it.

The older the Giants grew, the more they slept, ate, and drank, and the more their father disliked them. At length he told them one evening that they must go out into the world and seek their fortunes there.

" How are we to seek our fortunes ? " asked the three Billies.

" Go to Fairyland, get the three silver bells, and marry the three Princesses," answered their father ; and he turned them out of the tower, and locked the door upon them, without even letting them bid their mother good-bye.

" Do not fret, mother," said little Batty, flying out of the window after her brothers, " I shall bring them safe home."

" Batty," said Big Billy, " do you know the way to Fairyland ?"

"It is up a moonbeam," answered Batty; "but you are all three too big to get up on a moonbeam. You must let me go there alone, and wait here in the forest till I come back."

The Giants agreed to this. Batty got up on a moonbeam, and went off to Fairyland, whilst they stayed in the forest and went to sleep; this they did standing, each leaning against a tree; for as their father had no beds large enough for them, he had accustomed them to sleep so, resting against the wall.

When Batty got off the moonbeam this time, she found that she was close to the moon. She thought that it looked very dull. "I must see what is the matter with that moon," said she to herself. She opened it, looked in, and saw that it was sadly in want of cleaning.

"Well, I am sure," thought Batty; "I wonder at the fairies, I do, to keep their moon so untidy."

She shut up the moon again, and went to the King's palace. She peeped in at the window of a room in which the King and the Queen were talking together, and heard what they were saying. Fairies are such fickle creatures that they are always changing every-thing, and one of their great fancies is to widen or to narrow Fairyland as their whim may be. Now, the King wanted Fairyland to be widened, and the Queen wanted it to be narrowed that very night, for it is only at night when the moon is down that the fairies can do this, and that was what they were talking about.

"Fairyland is already too large as it is," said the Queen, "the fairies are always gadding about."

" I shall not widen it much," said the King, " I shall only take in the big oak in the forest to pass a review under it, and when the review is over, we can narrow Fairyland back again, and put the big oak out to-morrow night as soon as the moon is down."

The Queen agreed to this, and Batty having heard enough, got up on the moonbeam again, and went off to the forest. She woke her brothers, and making them stand against the great oak-tree, she bade them wait there till they found themselves in Fairyland.

" And mind," said Batty, " that you do not stir hand or foot till you hear the three silver bells tinkle, for once it is day the fairies cannot turn you out till night comes round again."

The three Billies, who knew how wise Batty was, promised to obey her, and in order not to be tempted to leave the great oak-tree, they went fast asleep as soon as they stood leaning against it.

The moment the silver bells rang, the King of the Fairies went to look at the tree, and the Queen went with him. When they saw the three Giants standing against the oak, and still fast asleep, they were amazed and disgusted. They did not know what to do with such big creatures, and they went home to the palace to consult together on the matter.

" That comes of taking in the great oak," said the Queen.

" Never mind the great oak now," said the King ; " but since we cannot turn these monsters out before night, what are we to do with them in the meanwhile."

The Queen said one thing and the King said another thing, and they were beginning to quarrel, when Batty, who was flitting near the window, put in her word.

" If you please, those are my three brothers," said Batty ; " and you can make them very useful if you like."

" And pray who are you ? " asked the Queen.

" If you please I am little Batty."

' Then show me your red mittens."

Batty showed her red mittens, and the Queen was satisfied. Still she said, "That is all very well, Batty ; but your brothers are too big to be of any use to us."

"If you please," said Batty, "I have seen that Fairyland is rather untidy, and my brothers could clean it up for you in no time. Besides you have been taking in a great many insects with the oak, ants, caterpillars, and the like, and my brothers will catch and destroy them every one."

The King and Queen did not much like that, but as they could not turn out the Giants till it was night again, they agreed to make them useful for that day.

When the bells had just done ringing the Giants awoke. Batty took them at once to the King, who set them to work.

"And be quick about it too," said the King; "for you have only this day to do it in ; out of Fairyland you go to-night."

The three Billies began cleaning up Fairyland, and hunting all the ants and caterpillars that had come in with the great oak ; but when the King saw the clumsy way they set about it, he cried out, "Stop, stop ; you

are rooting up all the trees, and treading on all the
fences. That will never do ! "

Then he called Batty, and scolded her finely for all
the mischief her brothers were doing. Poor Batty went
off to the three Giants, but she found that if the King
was not pleased with them, they were not pleased with
the King; for the moment they saw her they cried out,
" Batty, we are starving. The King gives us nothing to
eat but honey and dew. That will never do for us ; out
of Fairyland we go to-night."

" Ah ! but think of the silver bells," said Batty.

" We do not care about the silver bells," answered
the Giants ; " we want to eat."

" Would you like fish ? " asked Batty.

The Giants answered they would like anything that
was not honey and dew, but that eat they must.

Batty went back to the King. " May it please your
Majesty," said she, " I can see that the large fish pond
in front of your palace wants cleaning. My brothers
could clean it for you to-day, whilst you are reviewing
your army under the big oak tree."

" I don't know that the pond wants cleaning," said the
King.

" Yes, it does," said the Queen, "and Batty's brothers will do it beautifully."

So off the King and the Queen went to the review; and whilst they were away the three Billies cleaned 'the pond—and ate all the fish.

" Well, have you had enough ? " asked Batty.

"Enough !" said the Giants, "we are as hungry as ever. You must get us out of Fairyland to-night, or we shall starve outright, Batty."

Batty had something to do to persuade them to try Fairyland for one night more; and when they had agreed to stay, the King came back, saw that his fish was gone, and called Batty to give her another scolding. Batty begged his pardon, said her brothers were very hungry, and promised that they would never do it again.

" Of course not," said the King, " all the fish is eaten. Bid your brothers not stir from the oak tree, for out of Fairyland they go with it to-night."

" That is a pity," replied Batty, "for if my brothers go I must go too. Yet I see the moon is very dull here, and I could clean it up for you, if you gave me something handsome."

O

"Dear me," said the Queen, "clean the moon up! How nice that would be. The moon is dull, as Batty says, and we can scarcely see to dance at night. And how will you clean the moon, Batty?"

Batty said she would rather not tell, but she knew she could do it, if she got something handsome. "Something to take away out of Fairyland as a keepsake," said Batty.

The Queen was mad for getting the moon cleaned, and she persuaded the King into having it done that very night. She also promised Batty to let her take away whatever she pleased out of Fairyland.

As soon as it was night, Batty flew up to the moon, opened it, got in, and cleaned it thoroughly with her wings, till it was as bright as bright could be; and all the fairies who were looking on below clapped their hands, they were so glad to see the moon shine as it had never shone before. When the moon was quite clean, Batty came down to the King and the Queen of the Fairies, and dropping them a curtsey, she said, "Please, have I cleaned the moon to your liking?"

"You have cleaned it beautifully," said they, "and now make haste and mention the keepsake you wish

for. We like you very well, Batty, but we shall narrow
Fairyland as soon as the moon is down, and the big oak
and your brothers must all be back in the forest by peep
of day."

"Then, please," answered Batty, "I will have the
three silver bells in the belfry above the palace."

"The bells! our bells!" cried the King and the
Queen; "why, Batty, don't you know that we can
neither waken in the morning, nor eat at noon, nor
sleep at night if we do not hear our bells! Ask for
something else."

Batty said they had promised her what she liked, that
she liked the bells, and nothing but the bells would she
have.

"Nonsense," said the King and the Queen, "we cannot do without our bells, so you must think of something else that we can give you, Batty."

With that they went off to dance by the light of the
moon, which Batty had cleaned so well. All the fairies,
young and old, went after them, and the fairy who
watched the bells went to dance with the rest.

Batty flew at once to the great oak-tree, and bade Big
Billy come with her to the palace. When they were

there Batty got up into one of the bells, hung from the clapper, so that it should make no noise, then said, " Big Billy, take down that bell, put it on, wrap it round you, walk with it to the great oak-tree, stay there, and do not stir."

Big Billy did as he was bid. He stood on tiptoe, took down the bell, put it on, rolled himself well into it, then walked to the great oak-tree, and stood there as quiet as any mouse. Batty then got out of the bell, took Bigger Billy to the palace, and hanging from the clapper of the second bell, she made him take it down. This he did quite easily, being taller than his brother. Bigger Billy having put on the bell, wrapped himself well in it, walked off with it to the great oak-tree, and stood there as quiet as any mouse. When this was done, Batty and Biggest Billy went for the third bell, which he picked up, he was so tall. He put it on, wrapped himself in it, took it to the great oak-tree, and stayed there as quiet as any mouse, whilst Batty flitted about to see that all was right.

The Giants slept till sunrise, then they awoke, and called out : "Batty, are we out of Fairyland, and can we take off our bells ? we are so hungry !"

"You are out of Fairyland," answered Batty; "but you must not think of eating yet. You must keep on the bells, and walk straight on till you come to the palaces of the Princesses. You cannot miss the way; the bells know all about it. As soon as you are married to the Princesses, you may roof the turrets with the bells, but mind you do not roof the turrets first. And now I shall go and take a nod somewhere, for I cannot bear daylight, and I feel very sleepy."

The Giants did as Batty bade them. They walked straight on, and never took off the bells till they came to the palaces of the three Princesses, who nearly went wild with joy when they saw the silver bells they had wished for so long.

"Oh! you dear, good Giants," they cried, "what shall we do for you?"

The three Billies answered in a breath: "Give us something to eat. We come from Fairyland, where all we had was honey and dew, and a little fish."

"Poor fellows," said the three Princesses, "you shall have plenty to eat; but will you not roof our turrets with the bells whilst your dinner is getting ready?"

The three Giants were very good-natured, and they

did as the Princesses bade them. They roofed the turrets with the bells, then sat down to dinner. When dinner was over, and they had eaten enough, they asked the Princesses to marry them; but the Princesses only laughed at them.

"Marry you," said they, "who ever heard of Princesses marrying Giants! No, no: but if you will stay and watch the bells, we will give you plenty to eat, and that will do very well for you."

The Giants were rather vexed at being tricked, but they were very easy Giants, and they did not know what to do, so they agreed to stay and watch the bells.

When Batty had taken a long sleep, she thought she would like to know how her brothers were getting on. So she flew and flew till she came to the three palaces, and there she found the three Billies, not married to the Princesses, but each sitting in a turret and each watching a bell.

"Oh, that's the way the Princesses keep their word, is it!" said Batty; "well, I shall soon settle that."

Up she got on a moonbeam, for it was a fine moonlight night, and off she went to Fairyland. She found

" They roofed the turrets with the bells, then sat down to dinner."—*Page* 214.

the King and the Queen and all the fairies in such a
commotion as had never been, for the loss of the three
silver bells. As soon as they saw her, they all cried out:
"Oh! Batty, Batty, what have you done! You have
taken our bells, and we can neither waken, nor eat, nor
sleep till we get them back again. Only tell us where
our bells are, Batty, and you shall have three wishes
from us. Will you be a beautiful girl, Batty?"

"Thank you," answered Batty; "but I like flitting
about at night, and hanging from my heels in the day,
and if I were a beautiful girl, I could not do that; so I
think I shall stay as I am, if you please."

"Then, what will you have, Batty, to tell us where
the bells are?" cried all the fairies.

"Well," said Batty, "my brothers are very fine men,
but they are rather big. I should like them to be
shorter."

"Done!" cried all the fairies; "and now where are the
bells?"

"Wait a bit," said Batty, "my brothers are very good-
natured, but they are very stupid. I should like them
to be clever."

The fairies again cried "Done!" and asked Batty

what more she would have to tell them where the bells
were.

"I shall think it over," said Batty.   "As to the bells,
they are roofing the three turrets of the three palaces
belonging to the three Princesses who were to marry my
three brothers, but would not."

When the fairies heard this, they were as wild with
joy as the Princesses had been when they got the bells;
and as the moon was down, they widened Fairyland at
once; and the bells, the palaces, the Princesses, and
the three Billies were all in before you could have said
Jack Robinson.

"I declare," said Batty to her brothers, "you are no
longer Giants, but as handsome, well-sized, and clever-
looking men as I ever saw."

"Take off these bells and put them back in the belfry
of my palace," said the King of the Fairies.

"Yes; and we will keep the palaces lest any one
should be tempted to steal our bells again," said the
Queen.

"Just so," said the King; "and since the Princesses
were so fond of our bells, why they shall stay and ring
them for us."

When the Princesses heard that they were to remain in Fairyland for ever and ring the bells there, they cried and wrung their hands, and were distracted with grief, and begged very hard to be allowed to go back to the world again.

" No ; we cannot let you go," said the King. " And, indeed, I shall keep Batty and her brothers, too. Batty will clean the moon for us when it gets dull again, and her brothers are so clever now that they will be quite useful."

" Stop a bit," cried Batty, " you owe me a wish yet for telling you where the bells were, well then please to let my brothers and me out of Fairyland."

" Oh, please take us with you ! " cried the three Princesses to the three Giants. " Only get us out of Fairyland and we will marry you directly."

But it was too late.

" Done ! " had cried all the fairies, and in a moment Batty and her brothers were in the old tower again.

The Woodcutter and his wife were both as glad as glad could be to see their children.

" I knew travelling would do you good," said their

father to the three Billies ; and, indeed, the brothers were
so clever now that they got on famously and became
great men in no time.　Batty, too, was very happy ; but
she had her wish, and remained Batty all the days of
her life.

# Feather Head.

RINCE CRYSTAL and
Princess Crystal his wife were
a great Prince and Princess. They were very fond of
one another, but could never be of the same mind ;
for Prince Crystal was all for soldiering, drilling, and
fighting, and Princess Crystal was all for fiddling,
dancing, and merrymaking. When their only child—

a boy—was born, they both declared he was the loveliest of babies, but could not agree at all about the name they should give him.

"Let Baby have a fairy godmother," said the old King, "and she will settle that matter."

"The very thing," said Prince Crystal, "we will ask Poppy to name the child."

"Not Poppy," said the Princess, "she is spiteful; let us go to Fancy Tansy."

But Prince Crystal said that Fancy Tansy was stingy, and that Poppy was generous when she was in a good humour; "and if we take Baby with us," said the Prince, "she will not only give him a name, but present him with some fairy gift or other."

The Princess still wanted to have Fancy Tansy for the child's godmother; but the old King thought a fairy gift was worth having, and Prince Crystal had his way. The Prince and Princess found Poppy at home, but very much out of temper. The cat had got into her study, and spilt a fairy wash which she had been three hundred years in making, and which would have been the finest thing in the world for tan and freckles in two hundred years more.

"Well," said she quite crossly, when she saw the Prince and Princess and the Baby, "what do you want, and what have you got there?"

Prince Crystal told her what brought them, and asked her so politely to give a name to Baby that Poppy became more gracious, and answered quite kindly: "Come with me, and I will give Baby a name and something along with it."

She took them to the room in which she kept her fairy gifts. They were very valuable, but not all pretty to look at, and Princess Crystal was quite disappointed as she saw them.

"These are not things for babies, my dear," said Poppy. "Indeed, I have only three gifts left which would do for your boy — this pair of boots, this sword, and this cap ; you may take which you like best."

The boots were scarlet, and very pretty ; the sword had a gold scabbard enamelled with green ; and the cap was the loveliest blue satin cap that had ever been seen ; and though they were all the size just fit for a baby, "they were to grow with him and last him his life," said Poppy.

Prince Crystal looked at the sword. "I shall take that," said he.

"Whoever heard of a sword for a baby?" cried the Princess; "besides the cap is much prettier."

" Have the boots," said Poppy.

"Why so?" asked the Prince.

"Never mind, have the boots."

When the Prince and Princess heard Poppy advising them to take the boots, they made sure this must be the worst gift of the three, and the Prince wanted the sword and the Princess the cap more than ever. They nearly quarrelled about it, but Princess Crystal at last won the day, and the blue satin cap was put on Baby's head. Fairy Poppy was very much displeased that her advice had not been taken ; but she pretended not to care, and as they were going away, she took a white feather, stuck it in the Baby's cap, and said, " There now, you have had your way, and much good may it do you."

The Prince and Princess were scarcely out of the Fairy's palace when they remembered that Poppy had not named the child after all. She was such a touchy fairy, and so apt to take offence, that they did not venture to go back to her, but they began quarrelling as usual, each blaming the other for having forgotten the very thing they came for.

" It is all on account of that blue cap and feather," said the Prince. " I shall never call Baby anything but Feather Head."

" Well," answered the Princess, who was so pleased with the cap that she cared about nothing else, " I think Feather Head is as good a name as any."

The old King was delighted with the cap, and he agreed with Princess Crystal that it was most becoming to Baby.' Indeed, they both thought that he looked too well with it ever to take it off, so Baby kept his cap on night and day, for, being a fairy cap, it always looked quite fresh and new.

Feather Head grew up to be a very handsome and clever young Prince, but his temper was like the feather in his cap : whichever way the wind blew went Feather Head. He could never stay long at one thing, and when a fancy crossed his mind, he thought of nothing else, however wild and foolish it might be. When he took his hat off to have his hair combed and brushed, Feather Head became so sensible that no one could believe he was the same Prince, but the moment his cap was on again, Feather Head became as wild as ever. The worst of it was, that having always heard his mother say he never looked so handsome as when he wore his cap, he could not bear to have it off his head, and unless in very hot weather, he actually slept in it.

The old King and Prince Crystal died the same year, and Feather Head became King when he was just twenty. Princess Crystal at once went to see Fancy Tansy, who was her own godmother, and begged of her to give the young King some good advice.

"My son is the best, the handsomest, and the cleverest King," said she, "but he is always doing the most foolish things, and getting into trouble. If I say a word to him he laughs, and shakes his white feather at me, and looks so handsome that I forget what I meant to say, and if any one else ventures to advise or remonstrate, 'Hold your tongue,' says Feather Head, the moment he hears a word he does not like."

"I know," said Fancy Tansy, nodding, "it is all Poppy's doing, my dear; however, I shall look after him."

"Fancy Tansy is coming to see you," said Princess

Crystal to Feather Head, when she came home, "mind you are civil to her;" and Feather Head, who was a good-natured young King, promised to be very polite.

He was alone in his room one day when the window flew open, and in whisked Fancy Tansy in a little tortoise-shell car drawn by two blue griffins. The car being a fairy like its owner, immediately became so small that on alighting, Fancy Tansy put it on the table; and the griffins, fairies too, who were a sort of pony griffin, and remarkably diminutive, got under the sofa, and thence stared at Feather Head.

"Now, what are you doing?" said Fancy Tansy, for the young King was sitting back in his chair, his heels were on the table, and he was kicking at something, first with one foot, then with the other.

"Don't you see," answered Feather Head, "I am kicking that sunbeam."

"How silly you must be," said Fancy Tansy. "Feather Head, you ought to get married."

Feather Head did not like Fancy Tansy's fashion of coming in through the window, he did not like being called silly, and he had no wish to get married just yet; but all this he could have borne, if it had not been for

P

the griffins, and the way they winked at him with their little cunning black eyes, that seemed to say, " Come, now, no nonsense ; that may do for Fancy Tansy, but it will not do for us. Bless you, Feather Head, *we* know all about you." Indeed, these griffins provoked the young King so much, that though he went on kicking the sunbeam, he also tried to get a sly kick at them.

"Feather Head," said Fancy Tansy, "I see what you are at. Take off your cap."

"I won't," said Feather Head ; upon which the little tortoise-shell car grew large again, the griffins came out from under the sofa, and Fancy Tansy, car and griffins, all whisked away through the window.

The next time Fancy Tansy came in through the window in her tortoise-shell car and griffins, she found Feather Head sitting back in his chair with his heels up on the table.

"At it again," said Fancy Tansy; "now, what do you do that for?"

"I think you are always at it," said Feather Head, and he was going to add that he was kicking a sunbeam, when he caught the little griffins staring at him from under the sofa, and their little black eyes saying as plain as plain could be: "Come, none of your nonsense, Fancy Tansy may believe that, but we know better."

"Feather Head," said the Fairy, "I have got a beautiful Princess for you, and you must marry her."

"I don't mind if I do," said Feather Head, for he thought that if he were once married Fancy Tansy would not come so often ; but when the Fairy went on to say that the Princess was very rich and had this thing and that thing, he asked quite sharply, " Has she got griffins ? "

" Four," said Fancy Tansy.

" Then," said Feather Head, " I'll never marry her."

" Take off your cap," said Fancy Tansy.

" I won't," answered Feather Head, for he saw the griffins blinking and winking at him from under the sofa, and he felt so sure it was they who made all the mischief, that he got quite cross.

" Feather Head," said the Fairy, "if you do not marry the Princess I have got for you, and if you do not take off your cap this moment, you shall not see me or my griffins in a hurry."

" So much the better," cried Feather Head in a rage, " for I am tired of being lectured and snubbed by you and your griffins, and I will neither marry your Princess nor take off my cap."

The words were scarcely out of his mouth when the window flew open, and car, griffins, and Fairy were gone.

Feather Head never kept long of the same mind. Fancy Tansy was scarcely out of sight when he thought he might as well have married the Princess. He was sorry he had not asked her name, but when some one told him that Ruby was the most beautiful Princess living, he made up his mind to marry her if she would have him. Princess Ruby agreed to become his Queen provided he came to fetch her. Feather Head accordingly set off with a great suite, and travelled night and day till he came to the Princess's country. As soon as Feather Head saw Ruby he fell desperately in love with her, and the moment she saw him in his blue satin cap with the white feather in it, she declared he was the handsomest and the grandest King she had ever seen.

" Tell him to take off his cap," said the Princess' nurse to her.

" Oh, nurse!" answered Ruby, " that would be a pity, he looks so well in it."

" I don't like that nurse of yours," said Feather Head to Ruby, " and what are these black cats that are always after her?" For he thought the nurse's black cats looked like the blue griffins.

"Cats!" said the Princess, " well, they are cats to be sure. Are you fond of jugged hare?" she went on; " because I am, and, oh! Feather Head, I should so like a hare of your shooting."

" Then you shall have one to-morrow," said Feather Head, who knew he was a first-rate marksman.

Early the next morning Feather Head took a gun and went out. He had not walked long in the park before a fine hare ran past him. He was taking aim when the Hare said : " Why, Feather Head, what do you want with that gun?"

Feather Head answered : " I am going to shoot you, and take you home to the Princess."

" Why not catch me alive," said the Hare. "It will be greater fun, besides I am much handsomer alive than dead. Throw down that gun and run after me, not that I can run, for as you see I have a bad foot."

Feather Head looked at the Hare, and saw that she was limping; so throwing down his gun, he agreed to take her alive.

"Ah! but let us have some sport first," said the Hare.

"To be sure," answered Feather Head. "Start fair."

The Hare began leaping on before him, and Feather Head followed her close, but somehow or other, the Hare, though she limped sadly at first, limped less and less as she ran, and got farther and farther from Feather Head.

"You go too fast," said he.

"Nonsense," said the Hare; "keep up with me. I am sure you can if you try."

On hearing this, Feather Head did his best, but the faster he ran the faster ran the Hare, and the greater grew the distance between them. Feather Head became very hot, and thought he would take off his cap, which his mother had always made him fasten under his chin for fear of accidents; but when the Hare saw what he was about, she protested.

"Oh, Feather Head, how can you?" said she. "Why,

to see you running with that cap on your head and that white feather flying, is quite a treat to me."

"Very well," answered Feather Head, "I shall keep the cap on to please you, though I often wish I had never had it, it is so hot and uncomfortable at times ; but you must not run so fast, besides, you don't limp now."

"It is the running," answered the Hare ; "it has done me a world of good. I should like a run with you every morning, Feather Head."

"That can't be," said Feather Head ; "the Princess must have you to-day."

"Well, then, since this is to be our last run," said the Hare, "let it be a good one."

So off she went like the wind, and Feather Head, though no one had ever beaten him running, was soon quite exhausted. He threw himself down panting, and had only just breath enough to say, "Stop a bit, will you. I can't go on any farther."

The Hare replied that she did not mind taking a rest. So she, too, threw herself down opposite him, and lay nibbling the grass. When she had eaten enough, she asked Feather Head if he was ready.

" Oh, dear no," answered he.

When the Hare heard this, she rose, looked at him, laughed in his face, and leaped away. In a second she had vanished under cover, but Feather Head, who started up to follow her, could hear her laughing as she went, and all the echoes round said " Ha, ha ! " with the Hare, and laughed at him.

In his vexation, Feather Head tore off his cap. " Why, what a ninny I have been," said he as soon as it was off his head; "who ever heard of running after a hare ? No wonder she laughed at me." But the moment he put on his cap again to go back to the palace, he began to think he had not been so foolish after all, only a little unlucky. He was sorry, however, to disappoint the Princess of her jugged hare. " I must get her something else instead," thought Feather Head.

Feather Head never travelled without all his cooks. The moment he reached the palace he sent for them, and bade them tell him of some wonderful dish which he could cook himself for Princess Ruby. The head cook said one thing, and the under cook said another thing, and Feather Head disliked all their suggestions.

"Give me your cookery-book," said he to the head cook.

When Feather Head had the cookery-book, he read it all through till he came to the receipt for a sweet omelet: "To one gill of cream put four well-beaten eggs, sugar, cinnamon, and a pinch of salt, fry a nice light brown on a slow fire, sift fine sugar over."

"The easiest thing in the world," thought Feather Head, "and much nicer than jugged hare. I shall make it myself."

Feather Head asked for cream, eggs, sugar, cinnamon, and salt, then went down to the kitchen, locked himself in, and set about making his omelet. "The great thing is to beat the eggs well," thought he.

So he beat up his eggs, and was a long time about it. The shells gave him a good deal of trouble, for as the book said nothing about throwing them away, Feather Head took care to keep them every one. When he was tired beating up the eggs, he fried his omelet a nice light brown, as the book had said, sifted fine sugar over it, and sent it up to the Princess, with his compliments, and he hoped she would like it much better than jugged hare. The Princess sent back her compliments to Feather Head, and said she was very much obliged to him. But she was so vexed at not getting the hare he had promised her, that she would not touch the omelet. She pretended to have the toothache, and told her maids of honour they might eat it if they pleased. When the first maid of honour tasted the omelet a piece of egg-shell cut her tongue.

" What a delicious omelet," said she.

When the second maid of honour tasted the omelet, a bit of the egg-shell got between her teeth.

" Such a flavour," said she.

"Delicious! a flavour!" said the third maid of honour; "why, there never was such an omelet yet;" and she swallowed a large piece of egg-shell as she spoke.

When Princess Ruby heard them all praising the omelet so much, she thought she would like a bit.

"My toothache is better," said she, "give me just one little wee morsel to taste King Feather Head's omelet."

But the moment the bit of omelet was in her mouth, the Princess gave a little scream.

" Why, this omelet is made of egg-shells!" said she.

" Has King Feather Head done it to affront me ? I have a great mind never to look at him again."

" Well, it was too bad of King Feather Head," said the three maids of honour, " and if your Royal Highness were not so sweet-tempered as you are, you would never forgive him."

" Hold your tongue," said the Princess, " and go and tell King Feather Head to come up to me."

" My dear," said the nurse of the Princess, who sat knitting behind her chair, " tell Feather Head to take off his cap."

When Feather Head came, expecting to be praised for his omelet, the Princess scolded him, so that he was in despair.

" It is all the fault of that stupid cookery-book," he was going to say, when he caught the nurse's black cats peeping from under the Princess's chair, and winking and blinking at him as much as to say, " Come, now, no nonsense."

" My dear Ruby," said he, " how can you keep these hideous little beasts about you ? "

" Beasts ! what beasts ! you do not mean nurse's cats," said Ruby ; " she has promised me four kittens."

"They may be cats," said Feather Head, "but they look very like griffins, and I would drown the kittens if I were you."

This reminded the Princess that she was to tell Feather Head to take off his cap, but when she looked at him she found him so handsome with that blue cap and white feather that she could not make up her mind to do it. "I don't think I could marry him if he had not his cap on," thought Ruby, so she said nothing about it.

"And now," thought Feather Head, when he and Princess Ruby were friends again, "what am I to do? The Hare would not wait till I caught it, the stupid book never told me to throw away the egg-shells. What nice thing shall I get to please Ruby?"

Feather Head would have liked to get that nice thing for the next day's dinner, which was to be a grand one; but he could neither cook it himself nor let any one cook it for him, and so, though he thought and thought till his head ached, he found out nothing for the whole of that day.

The next morning Feather Head rode out, still thinking of the nice thing he could get for the Princess.

As he passed by a cottage he saw a beehive, and it so happened that he had never seen one before.

"What is that?" said Feather Head to his servant.

"A beehive, your Majesty."

"And what is there inside of it?" asked Feather Head.

The servant replied that there was honey within the beehive, but he did not say that there were bees too.

"Honey!" said Feather Head. "Why, honey is sweet stuff of course; it is delicious sweet stuff; I remember all about it."

And in a moment it flashed across his mind that Princess Ruby was very fond of sweet things, and that he could not do better than get that beehive and set it on the table for the dessert.

"But it must be a surprise," thought Feather Head; "not a word about it must I say till the time comes."

So he rode back to the palace without so much as giving the beehive another look. As he was going upstairs, he met Princess Ruby coming down, and when he saw her he could not help boasting a little. "Ah ha!" said he, "you still think about the jugged hare, I daresay, and about the sweet omelet, and you do not know what a noble dish I am going to have for you and your guests by and by. Do not ask me what it is, because I will never tell."

"Shall I guess?" asked Ruby.

"You may guess," said Feather Head, "but I shall never tell."

The Princess named many things, but she never thought of honey, and Feather Head laughed and was delighted.

When dinner time came round Feather Head bade his servant take the cloth of gold which he kept for state occasions, and follow him with four of his handsomest pages. He then rode off to the cottage, and bade his servant throw the cloth of gold over the beehive.

"May it please your Majesty," began the man.

"Hold your tongue," said Feather Head; "do as I bid you, and let my pages carry this beehive to the palace."

The servant did as he was bid, and the pages took up the beehive, and carried it off in state.

"Stop, stop!" cried a boy, running out of the cottage.

"Take that," said Feather Head, tossing him a purse of gold, "and hold your tongue."

"May it please your Majesty," said the boy.

"Hold your tongue," said Feather Head, and he rode away in a great hurry, and would not listen to the boy, who was only going to tell him that there were neither bees nor honey in the hive, which was an old one, but only a set of wasps who had got in there, and whom his father was going to burn out that very night.

"I think we will not wait for dessert," said Feather Head to the pages, "take that beehive in, and lay it on the table before the Princess."

"May it please your Majesty," said the pages.

"Hold your tongue," said Feather Head. So the pages did as they were bid. When the guests came in and saw the cloth of gold, they wondered what delicious dish was under it, and they all sat down expecting something they had never had before. Princess Ruby was very impatient to know what Feather Head had brought her in such state.

"Feather Head!" said she, "do get that cloth taken off, if you please."

"Take off the cloth," said Feather Head to the pages.

The pages took off the cloth, and the Princess and the guests stared when they saw a beehive.

"That is a beehive," said Feather Head to the Princess; "I daresay you had never seen a beehive before."

"Indeed I had," she answered very crossly, for she was quite disappointed.

"Well, I had not," said Feather Head, "and it is full of honey, and you like honey, I am sure."

"Yes, but I don't like it out of a beehive," said Ruby, still very cross; "and I do not like bees. Bees! why, these are wasps!" she cried, as a whole swarm came out of the hive, buzzing about the room, settling on all the dishes, and stinging the people right and left. Princess Ruby was one of the first stung, and flew out of the room screaming.

Well, there never had been at Princess Ruby's court anything like the disturbance there was now with these wasps. Every one pushed and tumbled against everybody else, and still more wasps came out of the hive, buzzing and stinging, till every one fled before them; and

" There never had been at Princess Ruby's court anything like the disturbance there was now with these wasps."—*Page* 240.

the room and the palace were full of them, and Feather Head was beside himself with shame and vexation. He sent for his servant, and threw all the blame upon him. " How dare you bring that beehive in here?" said he in a rage ; "why did you tell me there was honey in it when it was full of wasps ?"

"Your Majesty told me to hold my tongue," answered the man ; "besides I did not know there were wasps in the hive."

"Then the boy knew ; go and fetch that boy that I may have him hung," cried Feather Head, who was still in a great passion.

The servant went and fetched the boy.

"You knew there were wasps in that hive, and you never told me," said Feather Head to the boy.   "You shall hang for it."

"May it please your Majesty," said the boy, "you bade me hold my tongue."

"Then I cannot hang you," said Feather Head, "nor the pages, for I bade them hold their tongue, nor myself, for I am always doing foolish things, and I never know why, and all I can do is to go and beg Ruby's pardon."

Q

At first no one could tell Feather Head where Princess Ruby had gone to. At length, a little page said she was in a summer house that overlooked the sea at the end of the garden, and her nurse was with her bathing her face, on account of all the wasps that had stung her.

Feather Head went off at once to seek the Princess, but the moment he entered the summer-house, and she saw him, Ruby cried out, " Go away; I hate you. Go away directly."

But Feather Head, instead of going away, threw himself on his knees at her feet, and begged her to forgive him.

" I tell you I hate you, and your cap and feather," said Ruby, who had a very quick temper, and in her rage she snatched the cap off his head, and flung it out of the window into the sea. The moment his cap was off, Feather Head stared and burst out laughing.

" Well, there never was such a ridiculous fellow as I have been," said he ; " but if you will forgive me this time, Ruby, I promise never to be so foolish again."

" You may believe him, my dear," said the nurse, who

turned into Fancy Tansy, and was up in her car with the cats turned into griffins all in a moment. " Feather Head will be very sensible now. It was all Poppy's doing. Poor Feather Head, did you not know it was she who ran as the Hare, and laughed at you, and enjoyed your folly, and that she wrote that cookery-book, and kept the wasps quiet in the hive till it was on the table? But I was your friend, Feather Head, you may tell your mother so. Now, good-bye, and behave well, both of you, and Ruby has four griffins after all, Feather Head."

And away she flew through the air, leaving Feather Head bare-headed, but as wise a King as ever was, and Ruby with every sting gone from her face, and the loveliest four little griffins frisking about her.

" My dear Ruby," said Feather Head, "what beautiful little creatures these are."

" Oh, they are only kittens," said Ruby ; " but since it was all nurse's doing, I am very sorry I threw your cap into the sea, Feather Head. You do not look half so well since you are without it. I shall send a diver down for it."

Feather Head was in despair when he heard her saying this, for he knew what would happen if he got the cap on again. But though the Princess was obstinate, and sent ever so many divers down for the cap, and offered ever so much money to get it back again, no diver could find it for her, for when a fairy gift is lost or thrown away, it goes back to the fairy who bestowed it, and Feather Head's blue satin cap, with the white feather, had returned at once to its place in Poppy's palace, where it was quite ready for any one to whom the Fairy might choose to give it. Feather Head, however, never had it again. He married Ruby, and took her home to his kingdom, and became the wisest King of his day.

When Princess Crystal saw her son come back without his cap, she was inconsolable at the loss. It was no use for Fancy Tansy to tell her how foolish Feather Head had been whilst he wore that cap, Princess Crystal would answer : " That is very true, but it was the handsomest cap I ever set my eyes on, and I never saw such a feather."

Ruby, too, though she was Queen, and very happy with Feather Head, could not get used to him without his cap for a long time, and to the last of her days she was vexed with herself for having flung it into the sea. But Feather Head got on very well without it, and, indeed, he was so much afraid of getting it back again, for he knew how mischievous Fairy Poppy was, that he never wore a cap to the day of his death.